SONGS
of AGING
CHILDREN

SONGS of AGING CHILDREN

KEN KLONSKY

ARSENAL PULP PRESS
Vancouver

SONGS OF AGING CHILDREN
Copyright © 1992 Ken Klonsky

All rights reserved. No part of this book may be reproduced or transmitted in any part by any means without the written permission of the publisher, except by a reviewer, who may use brief excerpts in a review.

ARSENAL PULP PRESS
100-1062 Homer Street
Vancouver, B.C.
Canada V6B 2W9

The publisher gratefully acknowledges the ongoing assistance of The Canada Council and The Cultural Services Branch, B.C. Ministry of Tourism and Minister Responsible for Culture. The author gratefully acknowledges the assistance of The Ontario Arts Council Writers' Reserve.

Edited by Linda Field
Typeset by the Vancouver Desktop Publishing Centre
Printed and bound in Canada by Hignell Printing

"Songs to Aging Children Come" by Joni Mitchell
copyright © 1969 Siquomb Publishing Corporation

"Seth" first appeared in *This Magazine*. "Four I Love With All My Heart, Five I Cast Away" and "Horror Film" first appeared in *Education Forum*. "Reunion" and "Second Thoughts" first appeared in *The Sun* (Chapel Hill, N.C.)

CANADIAN CATALOGUING IN PUBLICATION DATA:
Klonsky, Ken, 1946-
   Songs of aging children
   ISBN 0-88978-253-9

   1. Teenagers—Fiction. I. Title.
PS8571.L6686 1992   C813'.54   C92-091577-9
PR9199.3.K66S6 1992

To Mary Ellen for love, endless patience, and wise editing; and to Ray for being himself.

CONTENTS

Introduction / 9

Seth / 15

Second Thoughts / 23

Jester / 37

Under the Bridge / 51

Past Life / 63

Four I Love With All My Heart, Five I Cast Away / 75

Three Solitudes / 83

Superintendent's Son / 99

Horror Film / 114

Reunion / 125

INTRODUCTION

ONE AUTUMN DAY WHEN I was fifteen years old, my mother left my father and me without as much as leaving a note. She had run off with another man.

I continued about my life as if nothing had changed—going to school, playing sports, and engaging in all the activities of a normal teenager of that era. I was naïve enough to believe that none of my school acquaintances knew what had happened, knew the shame I felt. Around that time I became more aggressive, more rebellious, lashing out in volcanic rage at everything and everyone. It wasn't until many years later that I began to understand that the conflicting feelings I had were a normal reaction to an event that would forever change my life.

When I was in my forties, I finally asked my mother why she hadn't written for over four months after she had left. It took that many years to prepare myself for the answer I had imagined would come: "Because I cared more about myself than you." As a teenager, I could not allow myself to experience the grief I felt at my mother's act of abandonment, nor could I interpret her action in any other way than that she did not love me. Even now, years after our reconciliation and her death, I feel a sore spot inside me, a sadness for that boy who was so hurt, confused, and angry.

◆

In 1975, I became a teacher of exiles and outcasts, students who were deemed unfit to continue in the mainstream of education. Their disruptive behaviours had resulted in rejection by classroom teachers and marginalization into special programs. In any of the several schools where I have worked, you will find a score of disgruntled teachers who say: "But for the rotten apples, this would be a great place to teach."

Oppositional, iconoclastic, I too, had been one of the "rotten apples." Something about school, with its rigid formalities, its incessant bells, rows of lockers and floors polished to a prison-like shine, provoked me to acts of defiance. In spite of, or maybe because of, my recalcitrance, I became a teacher.

I began in the profession with a strong academic background and a hope to transmit Shakespeare and the higher forms of culture to the better students. Like most teachers, I viewed disrupters as the enemy, a force which prevented me from performing my duties successfully. I did what everyone else did—I sent the 'problem' to the Vice-Principal. But the act of passing off problems began to sit on my conscience; teaching English no longer seemed the proper path for my own development.

In previous eras, when schools were crowded or boards of education less enlightened, difficult students were either eased out or expelled from school. As society changed, so did policy—now, everything was being done to keep them in the building—special classes for the disabled, the mentally retarded, the physically impaired, and the ones to whom I gravitated, the emotionally disturbed. The result of this policy, to the detriment of handicapped students, was segregated classrooms. While teachers were freed to teach the 'normal' student, the 'special' student was imprisoned with others who shared the same label. In the case of the students who always misbehaved, there were no longer any decent role models to choose from among their peers. Hence a great counter-pressure arose from both parents and students in these special classes to be allowed to integrate once again.

My present position, behavioural resource teacher, evolved from this game of educational ping-pong, this ebb and flow of ideas. My job now consists of helping disruptive students and their teachers live together in peace. Often the expectation of teachers is that I will somehow 'fix' the students, that I will magically make the problems go away. Many bridle at simple suggestions to alter the classroom environment or the curriculum, believing that change must come from one direction, from those least able to change.

Working with these students and in some sense sharing their 'outcast state' has forced a change in my perspective. When I pause to really look at them, I find that those faces reflect my own aloofness, the aloofness one adopts as a kind of protective barrier. When I stop to listen to the stories of these youngsters, I hear the hurt and loneliness of all rejected people. In turn, they teach me about the nature of our society and force me to take a closer look at myself.

The *Songs of Aging Children*, then, are stories which have come from the mouths and hearts of outsiders. Each story is a collaborative creation, mixing fictional occurrences with actual events. What the teller could not say, I invented from my own sense of shared humanity. The stories parallel my experience with the individual student, in each case attempting to get beyond the hardened adolescent to the vulnerable child. So difficult and draining is the endeavour to reach these people that it rarely meets with complete success; the victories are partial and few in number, the defeats total and devastating.

With more and more frequency, parents are unable to raise healthy optimistic children. Incidents of abandonment, racism, fatal outbursts of violence, and twisted sexuality have destroyed childhood itself. Trust has been replaced by anger and fear. The abused personalities who live among us have developed callouses which cover up the early wounds. Impossible, we say, that the monsters swearing at us were once innocent children. How, we ask ourselves, could such terrible things happen? In *Songs of Aging Children*, I have tried to provide a context in which the events portrayed become more understandable.

Adolescence is a time of uncertainty and incompletion. Much of the popular media would have us believe that teenagers are confident, beautiful, sexually competent individuals. The reality which I both see and remember is different. Almost every action of the average young person is plagued by doubts, misgivings, and feelings of inferiority. Such a mindset explains their notorious susceptibility to social pressure, their conformity; many cannot make a significant decision without their friends' participation and approval. Even more painful, then, is the position of the isolated adolescent who searches in vain for validation and reassurance.

The most noticeable feature of these young people is their inability to express certain emotions. Much like the adult male, emotion is expressed, but it is usually in the form of 'strong' reactions, such as anger, rage, hatred, and physical outbursts. Other emotions—tenderness, embarrassment, humiliation, love, grief—are often felt but seldom expressed as such, except to perhaps one favoured individual. A violent outburst often masks a soft, 'weak' emotion, thus allowing the teen to avoid exposure and the possibility of having to confront feelings which may be difficult to contain. Thus tragic or unpleasant circumstances are handled by a process of suppression and denial which can last well into adulthood. Perhaps it is these emotions 'held over' which cause some people to grow up to live tormented lives, unable to attain the level of emotional maturity which permits them to see the world and the people in it with understanding and compassion.

The title for this collection of short stories comes from a sad and wonderful song by Joni Mitchell, the words of which echoed in my mind while the ideas for the stories gradually germinated. The 'Aging Children' are those who are prematurely forced to surrender the preciousness of childhood. In the writing, which is based on many years of working with incorrigible and bitter young people, I had hoped to convey some understanding of the reasons for frightening antisocial actions. By helping others to empathize with a scorned and rejected group within our society, it might be possible to influence the cycle of vengeance and retribution which compounds the problem. In a world where it is so easy to look the other way, these stories offer the possibility for redemption.

Because my mother abandoned me as a teenager, I have considerable sympathy for adolescents in trouble. As a result of my willingness to listen and not judge, I am sometimes favoured with the truth, as when a fourteen-year-old told me he was responsible for his mother's wounding and his father's death because he had refused to accompany his father to the movies. That afternoon, the idea arose for *Songs of*

Aging Children, the idea that a heart which once more dares to trust might allow a devastated youth to reach out and take that next uncertain step toward adulthood. The moment when trust is reborn is nothing short of a miracle.

—KEN KLONSKY, 1992

SETH

THE DOOR TO THE BASEMENT is kept locked. It is a simple slide bolt. Instead of going to school on days when his mother goes to work, Seth slides open this simple bolt, opens the door, flips on the light switch at the top of the stairs, and descends. The scene, covered in five years of dust, is silent, intricate, and completely self-contained.

His father's stentorian voice remembered: "O-scale. I'll tell you what that means."

"I know what that means."

"That's one forty-eighth life size." A voice used to yelling above the steady drone of heavy machinery.

Seth peers into the train station window. Familiar friends are seated around a table playing poker. Frankie, opposite the window, hides his face beneath a blue-shaded visor. To his right is Red, a meaty moustachioed bloke with rolled-up shirt sleeves. Kid, a renegade cowboy hiding out, sits to Frankie's left, peering at the grimy lamp above the table, contemplating his next getaway. Seth is looking over the shoulder of a dapper white-haired gentleman, Bixby, holding three jacks, a four of hearts, and a deuce of clubs. Bixby's left hand sits on a pile of silver coins.

"The whole point, Seth, is it's gotta be real."

Beal Junction. Four minutes past midnight. A torn billboard above the track: a boy with freckled cheeks and slicked-down auburn hair holds up the familiar bottle and urges, innocently: "Drink Coca-Cola." Underneath the torn paper, another, older sign peeks through: the pink hem of a dress and the bottom of a large porcelain appliance.

The steely blue-gray Gore and Daphetid, due in at 12:30, is poised on its steep downward descent from an Appalachian Mountain tunnel. Bixby will confidently push his coins to the middle of the table. Frankie, having to service the train, will rise reluctantly from his seat and grab a lantern near the door. The train will pause for a moment at the station and then depart. The men will resume their game.

To talk of what will happen is to talk of what might have been, not of what is. His mother's voice: "He left you without a father, Seth, and for that I can never forgive him."

His father's warning: "Don't touch anything."

His eternal compliance: "I promise I won't, Dad. I'm just looking."

The power switch remains off; the train waits on the mountainside.

Beal Junction sits in cold serenity, a ghost town. One house near the rail station has a car in the driveway, a white fifties model convertible with huge fins, a Desoto. A lawn mower has been left out overnight to rust in the dew. 'Anderson' is the name on the mailbox. Is that Bud's car? Does their father know best?

A well-worn path from the mountain crosses and recrosses under the railroad track, leading to a crater with a small hole at the bottom near the centre of town. Father had built a waterfall and connected it to a pipe. Now, even the run-off has ceased.

Seth, long hair, jeans, black-and-white Led Zeppelin shirt, is, like Beal Junction, a throwback to an earlier era.

A sound. The car door. Audible only to one who is listening for it. Seth stands motionless, whiskers to the wind. He ascends the stairway in four practised leaps, shuts the light and slides the lock into place just as the front door comes open.

Mrs. Ribble, gangly and unkempt like her son, stumbles through the door holding two large bags of groceries, car keys dangling from her hand.

"Don't just stand there!"

Seth, catching his breath, takes the groceries from her arms and carries them into the kitchen, depositing them on the countertop. Mrs. Ribble limps in after him. The boy opens the refrigerator, pulls out a half-empty jar of peanut butter, and rips open a loaf of white bread which protrudes from one of the grocery bags.

"And don't be filling your face until you put away the effing groceries."

He eats. She fixes him with her good eye.

"Didn't you eat at school today?" Mrs. Ribble starts to put away the groceries. She puts a carton of milk into the refrigerator which Seth removes at the same instant to pour himself a glass.

"Didn't go to school."

"I don't want that old bitch calling me, you hear?"

"Hang up."

"They're gonna fine me."

"Bullshit, Mother."

"If'n you had a father, you wouldn't do as you do. I can never forgive the effing bastard."

To talk of what did happen is to talk of what is. What did happen is what will always be known as "the accident." Father enters the front door with two enormous Eaton's bags.

"Don't disturb me. I'm going downstairs."

"You got no business coming in here."

He pays no attention to her.

As her husband closes the basement door behind him, she says to her son, "That man is seriously ill, I want you to know."

Fifteen minutes pass. The basement door opens. The rifle barrel appears, butt squeezed tensely under the armpit, the face red and furious, blood vessels pulsing on the forehead.

Two explosions.

"What the fuck . . . . What the fuck?" Seth howling, tearing at his father by the shirt collar; a powerful backhand swing to the ear drops him, all nine years of him, on to the floor.

The next thing he hears: "Seth, your mother's still alive. I've called an ambulance. Just remember that I called the ambulance. I loved her. I love you."

And the next thing: one more explosion.

"Maybe if you'd left him alone . . ."

"Don't you go blaming me, you hear. He was effing crazy, is all. I ain't taking the blame. Half paralyzed me. Shot out my effing eye."

She points to it. That immobile glass approximation. Seth has never learned not to look at it.

"You couldn't leave him alone."

"You got a nerve blaming me is all I can say."

Seth finishes the glass of milk, pulls out a package of cigarettes from his shirt pocket, offers her one.

"Thanks."

He lights hers first, then his own. They both inhale deeply. Clouds of smoke fill the kitchen.

"Thank the Good Lord for these effing things.... Why didn't you go to school?"

"I didn't feel like it."

"You're ruining your life."

"Don't make me laugh, Mother."

Father worked in Oshawa. A good job. Steady work. Steady pay. Laid off only twice in twelve years. Put doors on vans. Every day. The passenger side door on Chevy vans. The era before the robots came.

One day he complained to the foreman. Couldn't take it any more doing the same thing day after day. Foreman changed his job. Every day thereafter until the accident he would drive every third van off the lot. Father was not a favourite.

"Get an education, Seth, or you'll take orders from people who don't know shit."

Every day he'd come home from work and head straight down the basement stairs.

"Going down to his trains," she'd mutter. "The man's crack-brained."

She'd learned not to go down there. Did her nagging from the top of the stairs.

"Ain't you gonna come up and eat some dinner? Ain't you gonna come to bed?"

Their tenth wedding anniversary she'd pulled out a recipe book and overcooked a roast. Before he went to work, she'd made him promise to eat with them that night. Forgot. Headed straight down the basement stairs. She waited. She went down. Lovingly. Reminded him. He didn't hit her. He didn't even look at her.

"Get the fuck out of here."

"Your father's a terrorist," she said at the top of the stairs. The tears ran right down onto her apron. She walked into the kitchen, took the roast out of the oven, carried it to the top of the basement stairs and slid the entire thing down, pan and all. Then she did the same with the mashed potatoes, the peas and carrots.

"Seth, you gotta make something of yourself."

"Mother . . . . "

"He never got no education either."

"He couldn't read."

"No, but you can. Why you missing school?"

"I don't know."

"You don't know."

"I just feel like I got no place to go."

"Bad enough he killed himself . . . . Also killed my son."

"What's that supposed to mean?"

"You talk like a dead man. Gimme another cigarette."

"Get your own, Mother."

"I should send you out to St. John's. Uncle William'd know what to do with you."

He left her or she threw him out the morning after their tenth anniversary. Seth heard the screaming well after the TV station signed off. He went out into the night, heard their voices finally disappear as he turned the corner on to the deserted main street. When Seth returned home in the iron-grey dawn, Father was gone.

"Seth! I don't know what's gotten into him. Seth, your father's on the phone. Seth!"

It's what he used to do as a baby. Tell her he'd want to speak to Uncle William. She'd call. He'd stare. "It's your Uncle William. Say something, William. That's your Uncle William. He won't say anything, William. Ma Bell's just loving this."

"Seth, will you talk to your father." Nine years old. He just stares. "He's got something special he wants you to do with him." She covers the mouthpiece. "He's gonna take you out. The man'll come unhinged if'n you make him wait any longer."

She holds out the phone to him. He moves his arm, begins to raise it, lets it fall. He shakes his head.

"Tell me and I'll tell him," she says into the receiver. "No, he don't wanna talk to you." She covers the mouthpiece. "Not that I can blame you . . . Yes? . . . He wants to take you to see *Jaws*."

"I saw it already."

"He says he saw it already." She covers the mouthpiece. "When?"

Seth just shakes his head.

"Says he'll take you to dinner too." She covers the mouthpiece. "More than he ever did when he was around here." She says to her husband, "I guess he's just not interested. I'm sorry. You try again. These things take time. Goodbye."

"Don't blame me for what's happened."

"I'm not blaming you, Mother."

She takes a cigarette from her son's shirt pocket and lights it off his. She drags deeply, implodes her whole face. " Just because your father had a mental disturbance is no reason to wreck your life."

"Mother . . . "

"I know, you saw the mess. How do you think I feel? I just want you to be something . . . . " She can't finish the thought. Tears stream from her eye.

"It's not because of him . . . and it's not because of you. Rest easy, Mother."

"Then who's it account of? Seth, I'm gonna scream if'n you don't tell me. Who's it account of you're ruining your life?"

"Me. It's on account of me."

"How so? . . . How so?"

"The day of the accident, that was the day after he called to take me to see *Jaws*."

She drags deeply. Looks at him. She knows that she is about to hear something new, but it is also something she has known all along.

"I hadn't seen the film, Mother. I wanted to see it."

"Oh no!" It hits her. "Oh no!"

"Next day . . ." he breaks off, unable to continue.

"Oh no! Seth . . . Seth . . . Seth." Her arms embrace him. He feels her tears on his cheek. Tastes her salt in his mouth. "You're wrong. It had nothing to do with you. Oh, my dear son. You been blaming yourself because you didn't go to some silly film."

"Yeah," he sobs. "If I'd've gone, I know he'd still be alive."

Then it hits her again. What he says is true.

"Oh no!" Each time she says it, the words are deeper and more painful. She feels a shortness of breath that threatens to overwhelm her. "It's because I made you afraid of him. He was trying to make it up to you, and I made you afraid."

He holds his mother as her arms drop. "Mother, stop. Stop crying. Please."

He leads her by the hand and she goes along as if inevitably. He takes her to the door at the top of the stairs, slides open the simple bolt, turns on the light and, hand in hand, they descend. Behind the billboard and the mountains is the power switch. Seth pulls down the lever and the scene comes instantly to life. The lights are muted and dull looking under the layers of dust, but the train rolls down to Beal Junction where Frankie and Red, dutifully as ever, emerge from the station house to service it.

"It's all in motion," she says.

"He wanted every piece of it to look real."

Gore and Daphetid has left for another long circuit of the Ribble basement.

"It was his true love, son."

"Did he love . . . me?"

"He did. He told you so. Of course he loved you, Seth. He could see how you worshipped the ground he stood on."

"Do you know there's five-eighth's mile of track down here?"

"No, I didn't know that."

"Gore and Daphetid."

"Don't say that."

"No," he laughs, "that's the name of the train. Sounds just like 'gory and defeated.' "

"Didn't know that either. I didn't know a whole lot. But then he didn't let me know."

"Do you know why he did it, Mom?"

"We smoke too much. Look at this basement." She takes a last deep inhale, throws the butt down, grinds it into the floor. "Remind me Seth, we have to quit . . . some day." One last cloud fills the air. She puts her arm around his shoulder. "We're stuck here together, aren't we?"

The train heads down the mountain, and once again the men go out to meet it.

"You see this effing train? It's the only thing in his life he could control. 'Cept maybe you. Some men are so miserable they have to control everything and everybody. Your father wasn't in control of nothing, not even himself."

"It's nice, Mother."

"Yeah, I'll admit it's a nice choo-choo."

"He had me. He had you. A good job. I don't understand. That's what I'm supposed to work for?"

Seth pushes the power switch back up. The train halts in some dark recess of the basement.

"Mother," he looks at her, grins, blows the hair out of his eyes, "just this one time, say something nice about him."

"How'm I supposed to? . . ."

"Please."

The train off, the cigarette out, there is nothing left to escape into.

"He spared you, Seth. He must've thought you could live better than he did. He spared you; I have to thank him for that, because I love you more than my own life, of that you can be sure."

"Thanks . . . . " He kisses her.

Trembling, she holds him to her. "Something makes 'em hate their lives, Seth." She hugs him, kisses him on the neck, the ears, any surface she can find. "Just please, will you please don't throw away yours no more."

SECOND THOUGHTS

I HAD SEEN THE BOY MANY TIMES before, but never really looked. I did not actually know his name until the day he was being escorted to the front office by a smug-looking vice-principal. He had finally 'gotten the goods' on this thirteen-year-old criminal; a set of school keys had been discovered in his locker. As I saw the boy go by, my impression was that he was from India. This impression, like many others to follow over the next three years, was false; it was attributable to the fact that when the boy was in trouble his complexion looked ashen, hinting perhaps at the fires burning deeply within him.

An amiable black police officer was waiting in the front office. He shook hands warmly with the vice-principal, and the three of them—the two large men and the small boy in between—disappeared into the office. I was able to learn from the secretary that the boy's name was Rico Papanou, and that this incident with the keys was the fourth time he had been suspected of stealing at the school, but the first time they had actually found 'hard' evidence. Suddenly, the vice-principal burst through the door, his face meat red, a purple vein throbbing on his forehead.

"I'll phone your mother and tell her to meet you down there." This was not said solicitously.

The police officer, however, was still smiling as he took Rico out the front door and into the waiting car and drove away. For him, evidently, the case was a lark.

Seeing me in the office and needing someone to talk at, the vice-principal said, "Lying criminal bastard. You know, Ted, when we get rid of all the bad apples in this place, we'll have ourselves a decent school. We actually found the keys in his locker and he won't even admit that he did it. He says that somebody must have planted them there. There's only two ways of handling a kid like this and I can't use either one; either take him out back and beat the shit out of him, or throw him behind bars and scare it out."

According to his records, Rico has transferred schools at least once for every year he has spent in the system. In the sixth grade, he saw the insides of four separate institutions. Teacher reports bristle with outright anger or, more typical, repressed anger gilded by the euphemistic language of behavioural psychology: "Rico has had an interesting stay at our school. He is a clever boy who must learn to use his intelligence in a more constructive and positive manner." He has also seen psychiatrists: "When asked to draw a picture of his mother, Rico asked the interviewer if she wished to see her in the morning or the evening. 'I wouldn't suggest you see her in the morning. She's pretty terrible in the morning.' The entire interview was indicative of just how unco-operative this boy has become."

Two days later, I'm getting into my car to drive home from school when I see him in the parking lot.

"Sir, you think I can have a ride?" So, he's been watching me as well.

I think to myself, "Do I really need this, especially after a full day in the classroom?"

"I go out to the highway," I tell him. "I don't think . . . "

"That's okay. Just let me off at the entrance."

"Look, Rico, I just want to . . . "

"Please. Come on, sir." His hands on the door, he stares at me, face pressed against the glass, features comically distorted.

"All right." I unlock the passenger door. "Where do you live, anyway?"

"Right there by the highway."

Since I've already checked the files, I know he lives two miles in the opposite direction. What does he want?

Saturday. South Scarborough. Driving along Birchmount Park.
"There! That's the place."
"Where?"
"It's back there. You missed it."
"What'd you say it was?"
"That's where I spent the first year of my life. Until she had second thoughts and took me back. It's a home, run by Children's Aid."
I've known him for two weeks and I'm never sure if what he says is true. The story about the home seems real enough.
"Why did she take you to Children's Aid?"
"She was ashamed when my father ran off." He smiles. It's the kind of pained smile one sees in a proud but beaten child. "They never got married."
"That's not so terrible."
"It's terrible to her."
"Where is your father now?"
"They say he works in Germany. I'm going to find out exactly where he lives. Then I'm going to pay him a visit. Then I'm going to kill him."
"Rico, you're going to waste your life thinking that way."
"He deserves to die."
We go to a hamburger place. The staff behaves as if it's on basic training with the U.S. Marines—very forced smiles and lots of rhythmical chanting. I find the use of my first name embarrassing.
"Order for Ted. Homeburger, salad, coffee with. Rico. Homeburger with cheese, fries, strawberry milkshake." It's repeated by the people up front.
"This place is fascistic," I whisper to Rico.
He likes this statement. He throws his right arm out, clicks his heels. "*Seig Heil!*" His loudness is even more embarrassing. The staff does not find Rico very funny. Neither do the rednecks behind us in the line.

"Let's take the food out to the car."

We sit in the front seat and eat. "You'll have to stop embarrassing me if you want this relationship to continue. I hate eating in the car."

"I love eating in the car."

"You'll also have to clean that pink milkshake off the upholstery."

"You're being very difficult, darling."

Despite myself, I laugh. "I think your mother must have been tempted to send you back a few times."

"More than a few."

"Why did she take you back home?"

"The same reason she sent me there. The Witnesses."

"What?"

"The Witnesses. They tell her what to do. They tell her what to think."

"Jehovah's Witnesses? You're Greek."

"I'm from Rhodes. There's lots of 'em."

"You don't believe in that stuff." Silence. "Do you?"

"Not really."

This hesitant answer disturbs me. "Let me explain something to you, Rico."

"Here comes the teacher."

"They let you die before they allow you to have a blood transfusion. What kind of people could let a child die for no reason?"

"There's something in the Bible about mixing blood . . . "

"Would your mother let you die like that?"

"Yes."

"That's crazy. It's evil."

It occurs to me that I'm tearing down the fragile walls of his life which, even at this moment, are no more substantial than a movie backdrop. What do I want?

Georgian Bay. The shallow aqua and deep blue waters, the white rock, white clouds blowing in a blue sky, the cliffs of the escarpment. Lion's Head. Along the bay and this entire side of the Bruce Peninsula are beaches of white dolomite, limestone rocks which, when you walk on them, clatter like potsherds. Their abundance is an embarrassment of riches to the very young, who are never sated by the simple act of throwing one rock into the water. Over and over we throw handfuls of these smooth white stones into the perfect blue of the water. They make a satisfying clap on the rock at the bottom of the bay.

The sun is amazingly warm when it finds its way through a space in the clouds. The contrast between warm and cold on this bay front reflects the discrepancy I feel between my apparent purity of motive and a certain residue of self-doubt. Rico, on the other hand, appears to be in that state of joy which is the sole prerogative of childhood. I watch him, and as another white rock arcs toward the blue water I imagine that he is whole again, that through me he has erased the damage of the past and started afresh.

Back in the cottage, I try to give him a reading lesson. For that, he has no patience. Instead, he kneels in front of the fire, poking the embers, throwing in logs.

"You gotta understand," he says abruptly. "My father is evil. I'm bad, too—you don't know how bad."

"Other people have said so. Not me."

"I am . . . . Promise you'll never tell this to anyone."

"You don't have to worry."

"No one. Not Melissa. Not anyone."

"It's in confidence. Complete confidence."

He waits.

"I promise. No one's going to know."

"She kept tissues all around the house. Everywhere. Boxes and boxes of the stuff. I could never touch anything without a piece of Kleenex in my hand or she'd hit me. Sometimes I'd forget and change the channel on the TV—my fingers touched the dial. She'd start hitting and screaming."

"God!"

"Yeah, God."

"I see what you mean."

"She hit me with a stick. She's never touched me. You can't touch her either. She's still the same."

"The tissue boxes and everything?"

"No, not anymore. I know not to touch."

Moved, and wanting to do something tangible, I get up from the rocker in front of the fire and embrace him.

"Rico, I love you. Maybe..."

"What?"

"Just maybe."

"What, darling?"

"Shut up. I don't mean it that way."

"Too bad."

"Rico! Stop! Listen to me. That's not a joke! What I mean is that you don't have a father..."

"And you don't have a son?"

"Right... and just maybe...."

There is a look on his face I will never forget. I have never seen it before: vulnerable, open. He can make no reply. For the first time in our relationship, he has nothing to say. Until this moment, we have been angling with uncertainty.

Now, every time he arrives at our apartment he has a gift, usually flowers for Melissa or feta cheese or overly sweet pastries.

"Where do you get the money for all these gifts?" Melissa asks.

"I'm working."

"I didn't know that."

"Don't give him the third degree, Melissa."

One night, he comes up empty-handed. Realizing that he has neglected to bring a gift, he starts out the door.

"Forget about it, Rico, I'll have to come down again to unlock the door for you."

"Just lend me your key."

"Okay, sure."

"Christ, would you look at this!" A colleague in the staff lounge is shaking his tabloid. "Bloody sods, the church is full of them, the schools are full of them. Listen to this one: 'Porno priest charged with pederasty.' Alliteration for bloody sodomites! Shoot the lot of them."

"That's really brilliant, Richard," I say.

"Your bleeding heart . . . " he sings, country with an English accent.

"Why don't you just shut up?"

"Aren't we being sensitive today." Then a change of tone. "Beware of Greeks bearing gifts, Ted. Certain to be spoiled goods."

I try to think of something to say without appearing defensive. Jill, an English teacher, is listening in.

"Richard is still angry with Rico for flattening his tires," she says. This saves me from replying.

New York. Battery Park. A March day, cold in the shade but surprisingly warm in the sun. In the haze across the water, a less-than-beautiful Statue of Liberty, under reconstruction, looks ironically like a prisoner inside her scaffolding. Sometimes, with a child, you do the things you never did yourself as a child, or if you did them then, you see them now with a double perspective, the naïveté of childhood and the cynicism of adulthood. For Rico, since he knows I grew up here, the places, the sights, even the traffic congestion are of inordinate interest. He takes many pictures with my camera, occasionally bothering to focus. He takes a full roll on the ferry approaching the Statue, another full roll at the Statue, and one more approaching the golden, sun-reflecting towers of Wall Street.

Later, we walk, endlessly. Chinatown, Little Italy, The Lower East Side. Trash and dust fly everywhere. We pass stained, worn tenement buildings, underwear and sheets flapping indecently on improvised clotheslines. The camera continues its frantic activity, collecting these exotic sights. Rico photographs a group of derelicts encircling a rusted, flaming oil barrel. They stare at us with hangdog expressions. Across the street an old oversized brown Pontiac careens out of control and smashes into a parked car. Pieces of glass fly in all directions. Click. A drug addict naps on a square of pavement as if it were a cozy bed in a warm garret. Click.

"Enough already!"

Click. Click. Click. I push him along.

We rummage through the stalls of Orchard Street and the shops with the never-ending sales of radio equipment and designer clothes.

I buy myself a ghetto-blaster and him more film, batteries, jeans, and sweatshirts. A voice rings out from across the street, three buildings north, from at least the second storey—a black voice, unmistakable, saucy. "Love child!" it calls.

Rico seems not to hear this impudent cry, even when it's repeated. He doesn't notice my reddened face.

"Let's get out of here."

"Why?"

"I've had enough of all this shopping. Come on."

My father, at whose house we've been staying, is clearly relieved when I tell him that we're leaving, lopping two days off the March break so that I can catch up on work. Neither he nor Rico actually believes this excuse, but for my father, at least, the real reason doesn't matter. The narrowing look in his eyes from day one has implied an unspoken question: "Why don't you give me a regular grandson instead of this?"

The drive home is somber, formal, distant. Rico spends much of the time hooked up to the ghetto-blaster, an annoying tinny sound issuing from the headphones.

Rico and I are supposed to go to the Bruce Peninsula for Easter weekend, but Melissa decides that she wants to go. Ordinarily, I'd hate to disappoint him, but instead I'm relieved. I promise him a future weekend, some time in May. He seems to take the news well. It's as if we were both beginning to disengage. He hopes Melissa and I have a great time.

The peninsula is unusually warm and bright for this time of year. We search for wildflowers. We visit the blue and white of Lion's Head where, desultorily throwing rocks into the water, I begin again to feel his presence.

Back in the cottage, there are traces of him everywhere: cards and a jar of pennies sit in front of the fireplace; an old jacket of mine he once used lies on the floor of the closet.

Even as we make love, Melissa senses an apartness.

Afterward she asks, "What is it, Ted? It's him, isn't it?"

"Yes."

"You love him."

"Yes," I hear myself say, without hesitation. "I thought I'd be able to, well—get away from him?" I end with a question because I want her to understand without my having to explain.

She slowly shakes her head. Her face is sad and amused at the same time.

"Can he live with us?" I ask. I realize that the idea has been inside me since the day I learned his name.

"Ted, I was happy enough to go along because I knew how much it meant to you, but—living with us?"

"Why not?"

"Just a hundred reasons. No privacy. We live in an apartment and he's an incredible snoop. I'll have nowhere to do my painting. What'll we do when friends come over? And what about his mother?"

"I think she'd be willing."

"Just to give him up? Just like that?"

"He's a lot of trouble . . . to her."

"You are just so desperate to have a child."

"Yes, damn it. So desperate. If only you'd put on some weight, like the doctor said . . . ." I trail off, having said more than I wanted to say.

"Then you wouldn't have to bother with him anymore."

"I didn't say that."

"Well, Ted, it's just never been that important to me, and it wasn't important to you either until this year."

"It's so easy when you live for yourself, Melissa."

"Don't pretend you're doing it for him." She turns away.

I soften my tone. "All right, then. For me. I want it. Would you consider a trial period? If any of us says no, the deal is off."

At least she doesn't refuse.

That brown stain on the horizon, Toronto. In certain areas of the city, such as our tree-lined street, the illusion of beauty persists. As we turn into the driveway, I see him at the front step with a blue knapsack on his back, waving a greeting. His face is ashen.

"Rico!"

"Thought I'd be here to help you guys unload."

"Great." I snap open the hatchback and step from the car. "Stick around. We'll order out some Chinese food and you can eat with us."

"Mother wants me to be home tonight."

"Really?" Despite myself, I'm jealous. "What's so important about tonight?"

"I just have to go, that's all."

"Okay," I shrug. Of course I think it's his way of emphasizing the distance I've put between us. Well, that can be fixed.

He helps to unload the car and pile all the stuff on the porch. Then he starts to head for the subway, turns around and comes back.

"I'll stay."

I unlock the door to our apartment and, as I enter the living room, I notice immediately that the ghetto-blaster is gone from its perch.

"Where's the ghetto-blaster, Melissa?"

"Wherever you put it."

I have a sinking feeling as I look around the apartment. At first there are no obvious signs of a break-in, but then I find that my spare car key has been taken. That's worrisome. Some bank books and tax papers have been ruffled through. Nothing else that I can see.

"Why don't you call the police?" says Rico.

"Yeah. I guess I have to."

The police arrive, clucking solicitously and offering tips on robbery prevention. After a perfunctory and fruitless inspection of the premises, one of the officers, a porcine fellow with a drooping black moustache and a heavy Scottish brogue, looks squarely at Rico and asks, "Who's this?"

"Don't worry about him," I say. "He's a friend of the family."

"You say the door was locked when you got home?"

Afterward, I send Rico home, as the robbery has upset me too much to eat. Stunned, I sit on the couch and stare at nothing. Melissa offers me a sip of her beer. "Have you considered that it might have been him?"

"What? What are you talking about?"

"Him . . . Rico."

"Stealing from us? Not bloody likely. That's ridiculous. I see what you're doing. You want to make sure he never lives with us."

"That's not true."

A deep freeze comes between us. We go to sleep. At 3 a.m., I awaken, feeling unusually alert. I walk over to the closet and reach into the back where we keep our camera. It's missing. I shake Melissa.

"You were right, of course. He did it. The ghetto-blaster, the car key, the camera—he must have taken the camera. God, am I a fool! And the cops were here. He probably had it all in his knapsack. What cheek! The covetous little bastard must've gotten the key to our apartment copied."

Melissa is barely awake. I'm not even sure she's heard what I've said.

"I'll call him. He'll give it back. He's got too much to lose."

The Broadview subway station. I said nothing specific on the telephone, but he must have known from my voice that I am disturbed. I wait five minutes and he emerges from the station door, smiling a bit less than usual, but smiling nonetheless. We drive over to Withrow Park, sit on a bench. It is a perfect evening, cool and very clear.

"What's this all about?"

"I've thought about it—what you did, Rico—and it's understandable, but . . . "

"What are you talking about?"

His feigned innocence is predictable but still infuriating.

"You don't have to pretend. You took the stuff. The radio, the key, the camera. Just return it."

He says nothing.

"We'll continue on just as before."

"I didn't know about the camera. They got the camera?"

"You did."

He puts a hand on my arm. "Ted, I didn't do it."

"You did it. Just give it back."

"You're wrong . . . . "

I believe he could outstare the devil. He's incredibly brazen.

"Do you think I could do that to you?"

Against my will, he forces me to review the evidence inside my head.

"You did it, Rico. I can forgive you. Just give me back the stuff."

He sits and smiles at me, as if he were completely innocent. I suddenly remember the vice-principal and the keys. A repeat performance—but to me! To someone who dared to love him, not some uptight school official.

"Rico, we were going to take you in to live with us." I'm on my feet, walking away.

"Can you give me a ride?"

I don't even look back.

A government housing project in Scarborough. Very high. Very wide. Three monoliths. The Papanou apartment is much larger than I expected. The walls are bare, the fixtures and furniture tacky. A framed photograph of Rico smiles from an otherwise empty bookcase. The place is abominably filthy. Cockroaches wander unmolested on the kitchen walls and the counters.

Mrs. Papanou is a very small woman with black hair cut like Cleopatra's. She keeps a wide distance between herself and me and, as Rico has said, between herself and him. I conclude that the condition of the apartment is the result of her not wanting to touch *anything*.

"Does not matter what I say to him," she says, "Rico, he won't do nothing I tell him. Sit up straight."

Rico moves a bit on his chair.

"You see?"

"You don't have to return the stuff, Rico. You probably sold it or threw it out. I'm just going to ask you to do one thing." I pause for effect. "Just one request."

"Sit up straight. Listen to Ted. Nobody ever does nothing for you before. I'm sorry this happen. What do I do with him?"

"Rico, just admit you did it. That's all."

He sits. He smiles. He stares.

"I can't have a relationship with you if you continue to lie to me."

"He does steal before—many times. He stealing from me all the time. But this, I don't know. He tell me he does not do this thing. I never see these things you talk about. Maybe he tell the truth this time?"

"He doesn't tell the truth this time, Mrs. Papanou. He doesn't ever tell the truth." Another pause. "Rico!"

He shakes his head. "I didn't do it."

Melissa is on the living room couch trying to sleep, legs propped under the pillow, one hand on her forehead, the other on her expectant womb. The telephone rings.

"Hello." Eerie silence on the other end of the line.

"Take it off the hook, Ted. I'm getting the creeps."

Minutes later the phone rings again.

"Ted, I feel sick," Melissa calls out. "Take it off the hook."

I pick up the receiver. "Hello? Rico? Listen to me. I'm going to call the police." This time, when he hangs up, I leave the receiver dangling. "We're getting an unlisted number."

A terrible sadness inundates me, a feeling of suicidal sadness when all I should be feeling at this time is joy. Melissa sees my pain. With great effort, she rises from the couch and comes over to comfort me, stroking the back of my head.

"Ted, you tried. You tried to reverse the irreversible. Please. Please just try to forget about it."

"Why?"

"Because it's hopeless.... And we have other things to think about."

"No, I mean why did it get messed up like this?"

"Who cares? I mean who fucking cares? I'm giving you a child. Isn't that enough?"

She's crying again. Lately, she has been breaking into tears at the slightest trifle. A result of pregnancy—so we've been told. This time, I comfort her. I walk her back to her place on the couch.

"It's *our* child," I say.

"Oh, I know, I know, and I'll love it—unconditionally, despite whatever I've said. Whatever it's like, whatever it does, I'll love it, because I've seen what they turn into when you don't."

"Whatever he does..."

"Or she."

"No, I'm thinking of Rico. Don't you see that's where I failed him?"

"Ted, I don't want to hear about somebody else's messed-up kid anymore."

For the first time, what Melissa has been telling me all along is too plain before my eyes. I put too much trust in him, not wanting to face the angry, needy child, because the reality had little to do with the image I was creating. It was more important that I *see* the truth than that he be forced to *tell* it. The only difference between me and all the others—his mother, the vice-principal, his father, all those who have left him, rejected him, or cast him out—is that I saw an angel when they saw a devil. What we all would have seen, had we looked, was a soul in torment. I wanted only to possess him, to steal the precious name of son from his mother, just as he stole in order to possess me. An act of love is nothing like that—surreptitious, hoarding, greedy. I am afraid, yes, of what others think, but I am even more afraid of love, love that requires you to continue loving even when you've been hurt.

"Melissa, you're not going to like this, but I'm going to call him again."

She sighs.

"I mean, I just can't leave him out there like that."

"Ted, do what you want."

"Yeah, I'm going to call him." But I don't.

Oh, god of love, save us from our fear.

JESTER

KRISHNA HAS ONE FANTASY which he shares only with his sister. He imagines he is standing before the bathroom mirror with a razor blade. He slices his skin paper-thin in a line along the collar bone and begins to peel off the ash-dark outer layer up the neck, beneath the chin, and all the way to the line of dark hair along the forehead. What is revealed beneath the layer of dark skin is the lightly tanned face of a white boy.

"I'd be damned good looking then, wouldn't I?"

Najma studies her brother's features reflected in the full-length mirror of his closet door: eyes like deep blue agates, wide yet slightly aquiline nose, soft pinkish lips, hair like a rock singer's—long, dark, falling down his shoulders in wavy ringlets, stooped posture making him appear shorter than he actually is, bare chest and white track pants.

"You are a very good looking boy." She adores her brother through the wide eyes of a sheltered fourteen-year-old. Since Krishna has quit working in his father's store, his mother and he have had to switch places. She went to work selling nuts and spices and he has looked after Najma. In every other way he defies his upbringing, but his attitude toward women is a perfect reflection of the Guayanese immigrant community. He guards his sister zealously, restricting her social contacts, and forces her to account for every minute late. She has become restless under this prison-like regimen, but continues to accede to it more out of love than fear.

Krishna stares at his image with distaste, a pained grimace distorting his features. He digs his comb into the blue-black hair, turns away from the mirror and puts on the rest of his clothes.

"Daddy says you should cut your hair," says Najma.

Krishna stares out at her as if peering through the dense undergrowth of a forest. A small hiss escapes his lips.

A car horn honks in tune to 'You Are My Sunshine.' Charlie has arrived in his refurbished purple van to pick up Krishna for a party. Najma likes Charlie because his presence seems to be the one thing that always makes her brother happy. Charlie will also talk to her. He is not one of the kids who yells "Paki" in front of their townhouse at night.

"Good night, little one," Krishna says to his sister. "You be a good girl." He points his finger at a forty-five degree angle, a gentle warning gesture he has seen his father use, halfway between pontification and accusation.

Krishna gets into the van, Charlie's second home. There are two cases of beer on the bed in the back and a bottle of cheap rye on the floor of the passenger side. He learns that Trish, Charlie's girlfriend, is going to meet them at the party. "She'll be bringing a friend who I happen to know is pretty good looking."

"I hope she's better than the last one," says Krishna, as he picks up the bottle of rye.

"She is, I guess. Hey, the last one wasn't so bad." Then he says, pointing to the rye, "Not in the car, Kris, I'll lose my license."

Reluctantly, Krishna lays the bottle on the floor again. "Trish would never bring a girlfriend better looking than herself."

"What girl would, buddy boy?"

Krishna, trying not to think of the bottle, shifts his attention to the darkened street outside the van, one of Scarborough's cavernous plaza-lined avenues. All of the ancient, inconvenient trees have been bulldozed, leaving a handful of pedestrians exposed to a razor-like wind. A red light draws his attention to a bus stop where an overaged hippie, a black woman, a young couple, an anesthetized kid with a head set, and three old people in protective postures wait. Except for the young couple, the group seems passive, staring off in all directions, but Krishna knows they would sooner acquiesce to a rape or a murder than allow someone to jump the queue. The couple, unconcerned by the cold, is lost inside each other's eyes.

Krishna, envying their love, contemplates the evening ahead. Jeff's parents have gone to their cottage for the weekend. Of course his parents warned him not to have a party in their absence, but a friend or two is not a party, and word tends to get around quickly. There is no telling how many kids will actually show up, but Charlie is a football hero; merely a rumour of his presence is an assurance that many others will be there. These parties fill Krishna with tension and dread, but he attends them because he loves Charlie and craves the distinction of being his friend.

Krishna was invited to spend part of the last Christmas holiday with Charlie's family. He remembers the fire, the dark wood, the silvery decorations. Amidst hunting and golf trophies, his parents seemed dignified, friendly, and civilized, drinking brandies with the two boys and asking Krishna questions about his home life, his past, and his future. So what if his answers were filed and polished? To such people, the truth was irrelevant; the only thing that mattered was sustaining the polite conversation. "This is how I want to live," he thought. Then, late on Christmas night, Charlie's father, noticing the pizza crusts and soft drink cans in front of the television in the den, scowled like Alastair Sim as Scrooge and spoke icily to his son, "Get that crap cleaned up, Charles." For weeks, Krishna has mulled over the father's abrupt change. Why did he have to say it that way?

They turn into one of the housing developments which sit behind each plaza. All the streets are winding crescents and laneways, each house on a large plot with a two-car driveway. Jeff's house is at the circular end of a small lane with no sidewalks. Charlie pulls behind six other cars already in the driveway, the rear end of the van protruding into the street.

When they enter the house, there is shouting, swearing, and threats of violence in the kitchen. Jeff, the anxious host, is trying to calm the combatants, but is instead being drawn into the eye of the storm. What is it about? Girls? Betrayal of secrets? Krishna is reminded of Act III, Scene One, in *Romeo and Juliet* which, as his favourite English teacher had said, "shows us the dangerously short fuses of the young."

Charlie has put his arm around one of the arguing boys and starts telling him a joke. It is not only his good nature which defuses the situation, but his quiet strength as well. Charlie moves him out of the kitchen without the boy's full awareness. Had he tried to resist Charlie's direction or had he persisted in the argument, he would have felt the greater weight behind the benign and friendly gesture.

Krishna empties one of the cases of beer into a large cooler filled with ice, takes a cup, and goes to work on the rye. He stands near the cooler in a corner of the kitchen, strategically placed to greet most of the guests.

"Hi, Kris." Paul extends his hand. On his left arm is his girlfriend, Kim.

"Hey, Paul, how ya' doing?" Krishna shakes the indifferent hand as Paul quickly glances down to the cooler. Paul opens a beer and places it gently into Kim's mouth. She pushes his hand away, takes the beer, and does likewise to him. Then she opens one for herself. Krishna feels they are performing for him just as when he smiles back he is performing for them. He has a sudden urge to say "assholes" right to their faces, but they pass on quickly to the living room.

Drinking furiously, Krishna's hold on himself begins to weaken further. Pulling a beer from the ice and opening it, he hands it to a red-haired girl suffering from the facial scars of adolescence.

"To the beauteous Roxanne!"

Roxanne accepts it gracefully, forcing a smile to her round face. Tears are visible in her eyes. She turns away.

"Andrew, keep yourself in hand tonight." He says these words to a large boy whose frustrated lust and failed attempts at dating are legendary. It is common knowledge at the high school that Andrew must often switch classes hiding an erection behind his books.

"Shut up, Krishna." Andrew has chosen the one effective retort, the use of his actual name, a reference to his race.

"Of course, there's an empty room at the back of the house if you get lonely."

Andrew throws his beer bottle at Krishna who ducks as it shatters behind him in a spray of foam and glass. He starts toward Krishna but is stopped by Charlie's arm, the enforcing arm of the peacemaker, ever alert to trouble.

"Why do you bring this Paki with you everywhere?"

"He's my friend."

"Well, tell him to shut his mouth! He's got a big mouth . . ."

"So do you, Andrew."

"... for a Paki."

"See what I mean?" Charlie's right fist slams into the conjunction of mouth, lip, and nose on the side of Andrew's face. At first, there is a distinct pause; Andrew is still as stone. Krishna has the instantaneous impression that the punch never happened. The pause breaks. Andrew takes one step toward Charlie and then three steps to the right. From the left side of his mouth and from both nostrils blood pours. Andrew crumples to his knees. A visceral thrill shoots through Krishna's body.

"Looks like Andrew's going to be on the shelf a few more weeks," says Krishna.

"I hope you have eyes in the back of your head." Andrew spits this comment squarely and solely at Krishna, stated and sealed with his own blood. "You're gonna need them." The jester feels a sober chill go through him.

"Kris," says a voice. Trish, Charlie's girl. "Who did that to Andrew? Not you?"

"No."

"Charlie?"

Krishna nods.

"Charlie!" A peace activist, Trish hates violence but loves Charlie. She has been able to reform him to the degree that now he usually confines his violence to the football field. However, she finds the outright bigotry of many of his friends an even greater sin. Hence, when Trish learns of the reason for the punch, she softens. She fills a plastic bag with ice and applies it to Andrew's broken face. Charlie comes over and helps Andrew to his feet and the couple together guide him into the living room.

From the other side of the kitchen, Krishna hears his name spoken. He strains to listen to the conversation, catching one line: "Charlie would do anything to keep her happy."

Unable to fully absorb the implications of this statement, Krishna is distracted by a familiar face in front of the cooler. Ranee. Her family and his are well acquainted. Shapely, confident, assertively intelligent, she is also a transplanted Guayanese Indian. For her to attend such a party is an enormous risk, considering their insular world. Her busy

hands remind him of a novice comedian who has just told a bad joke. Then comes a dawning realization: it's Trish's girlfriend, his date for the night. As she awkwardly attempts to smile at him, he turns away.
"Hi, Krishna." He winces as she crushes the *r* in his name.
"How could you come here? Look at the way you're dressed!"
"I changed into jeans at Trish's house. We are supposed to be studying."
"Then go study."
"You're talking like an old fart."
"You two know each other?" Trish has come back into the kitchen to make the introductions.
"How could you bring her here?"
"Huh?"
"This is no place for her. What a stupid thing to do!"
"Kris, you've done nothing but drink at all the parties we've been to. Just stood around and gotten drunk. I thought maybe you'd want to meet someone . . . " Trish's abrupt halt is prompted by a sudden understanding of Krishna, realizing that if she goes on she will compound the unintended injury already inflicted. But it's too late. Krishna finishes her sentence in his mind. He picks up the bottle of rye, now half a bottle, gulps down as much as he can in front of the two girls, and staggers past the hash smokers in the doorway into the night.

Out in the middle of the road, he stumbles to the end of the laneway. In his eyes, the streetlights shimmer like asterisks.
"Kris!" He hears a voice like a dream trying to awaken him. "Kris!" A great white shark with glaring eyes approaches. Krishna is mildly aware of the horn and the screech of brakes, unconcerned that a large car has missed him by centimeters. "Kris!"
"Get that jerk out of the road before he gets himself killed!"
Krishna feels a sudden loss of volition, the sensation of being carried like a baby, and the caress of cool grass on the back of his neck. A weight falls on top of him, a pleasant feeling of being pinned to the ground.
"Kris." Charlie's voice. Then nothing.

❖

Unwanted light awakens him. Then he sees a pair of wide almond eyes filled with tears: Najma.

"Krishna!" His mother's harsh voice. They have invaded his bedroom. He has an overwhelming urge to pee. "You're coming in drunk all of the time, throwing up over everything. . . . " Her voice goes on. A ripping pain sears his forehead above the right eye.

The late winter sun through the opened shade creates a glare off her bright red sari. The red *kumkum* on her forehead, the voice, the accent, grate at him. "Why don't you just stop talking?" Krishna escapes to the bathroom and locks the door. He relieves himself and then gulps down three aspirins. Instinctively, he turns his face away from the mirror. What did he do last night? Can he appear at school on Monday without embarrassment? With a shudder, he remembers: Ranee, Charlie, the words of warning.

He looks again at the mirror, repeating with insistent voice the words of a bothersome school counsellor. "You're nineteen years old, young man. What are you going to do with yourself? Have you thought about a career?" His answers to these dreaded questions have been facetious: "I want to be a fireman." "I just want to have some fun before the bomb drops." On one occasion he tried to get serious, mumbling something about going into advertising because he is a skillful writer. The counsellor pulled out career charts, pamphlets with college training courses, list of contacts, and Krishna opened his mouth and let out a huge yawn. End of interview.

"Krishna, other persons in this house are waiting to make use of the bathroom," says his father with his usual polite formality. Krishna understands the urgency, knowing that Saturday's till is three times heavier than any other day. The family store sits out on Gerrard Street East in an area where all of the businesses and restaurants are owned by Sikhs, other Indians, Pakistanis, or Guayanese. Many of the owners are highly educated—engineers, professionals in their country of origin—but willing for the sake of their children to be storekeepers in Canada. Krishna's father was a good doctor but, like dozens of those other storekeepers, did not have the time or the savings to 'upgrade' his qualifications. Prevented in this way from practicing medicine, he has become a good storekeeper.

Krishna used to love the pungent aromas and the casual ambience of the store. The work—unloading the truck, sorting the goods, filling the shelves—was hard but enjoyable, allowing time for conversation with people in the community. One day a small group of students from his school happened to see him carrying a box of mangos into the street. He felt too ashamed to even ask what these suburban kids were doing in this area of the city. They, of course, saw his uneasiness, and he felt a flash of heat behind his ears, felt as if he were standing in his underpants with a box of mangos in his arms. He would not come to the store after that day, and he could never explain the reason to his father.

He emerges from the bathroom. "Good morning, Krishna. Your friend brought you home last night and not in good condition."

"Good night, Dad." His father's voice pleading with him to spare a Saturday at the store is what he hears as he pulls down the shade, slips beneath his still-warm comforter, adjusts his head on the soft pillow, and falls back into a deep tranquil sleep.

✧

On Friday, Krishna comes to school late, has in fact decided to come only to mollify his father. Krishna had planned to spend the last day of the week, as he had done the two days before, drinking, but he made no secret of his habit, not bothering to hide the empty bottles. His father had learned not to interfere as long as Krishna was able to look after his sister, but on this day, choosing to notice his son's steady deterioration, he took a stand. He threatened, as he did every so often, to throw the good-for-nothing out of the house if he did not start to pull his weight at school.

Krishna enters the school through the back door and wanders the empty hallways, occasionally spotting a teacher lecturing in front of the room or sitting at her desk. The students, some paying attention, some with glazed eyes, some waving to him, some drowsily doodling on desks, give a clear and soundless indication of the level of interest. In the front office, he signs in the late register under the watchful eyes of a large dour secretary in an electric green sweater.

On his way to class, Krishna passes the gymnasium where he hears the pop and flutter of badminton birdies and by force of habit looks into the open door expecting to see Najma. She is not there. Uneasy in his mind, Krishna begins to climb the stairs on his way to science class when he catches a glimpse of the hair and shoulders of an amorous couple beneath the stairs. The hair and the singsong rhythm of the voice are unmistakably his sister's. He stops dead on the first landing. They are oblivious to his presence. He hears an escalation of arousal, the clicking of tongues, the quickening of breath.

Just then, the hallway door squeaks open and a woman's harsh voice calls out: "Andrew! I assume you have a class this period! What are the two of you doing here?" As he enters the upstairs hallway, Krishna's racing mind can only focus on an irrelevancy: the Principal does not know his sister's name. Appearing without books or purpose, he enters his science class and takes a seat in the back of the room. Mr. Gizzy, the teacher, rolls his eyes for the benefit of the other students. Krishna pretends to pay attention, but is shaking with inner turmoil. "So this is what Andrew meant: Najma." To date, his guardianship of his sister is the one area of his life where he has not been forced to hear the disappointed groans of his parents.

Staring at the blackboard drawing, the anatomy of some one-celled animal, he slowly forces himself to concentrate. He must find Najma as she goes into her second period class, take her outside the building under some pretext, perhaps that "Daddy is sick," and have a talk, reminding her that her father would sooner pull her out of school than allow her to socialize.

He rehearses the scene between them over and over as the science lesson drones on. Mr. Gizzy, seeing Krishna become increasingly distracted, calls upon him to answer a question, but Krishna is not even aware he is being addressed. The science teacher is in mid-sentence as the bell rings, but Krishna, to the amusement of the class, runs out the door.

The dour secretary waits at the front desk, a formidable fire-breathing dragon. When Krishna asks her for his sister's timetable, she suddenly remembers a waiting telephone call. Furious, the young man reaches over the counter into her lair, grabs the timetable book, and starts flipping through the pages.

"Hold the line, please," she says into the telephone, then covers the receiver. "Just what do you think you're doing?"

Krishna finds his own timetable, turns the page and locates

Najma's. Room 229. English class. Without bothering to close the binder, he flings it across the counter at the dragon. "You wouldn't treat a white person that way!"

Many of the students have already taken their seats in Room 229, but not Najma. Krishna waits at the door, now shaking visibly. Latecomers stare at him, then file in. The teacher, Ms. Robinson, the Shakespearean who was able to capture Krishna's interest last year and who is aware of his drinking problem, asks him if he is all right. Krishna is not able to speak; he just shakes his head from side to side. "Come back after class; we'll talk about it." The door shuts, and he dimly hears her call the class to order. His mind keeps going back to the party.

"Shit!" This scream, a cry of despair, is heard up and down the hall. Some doors open, faces peer out. He goes downstairs to call home, hoping by some miracle to hear her voice. His hand is jumping so much he has to try three times before being able to push the right numbers. Five, six, seven rings. No answer. Only one conclusion seems possible: they must be at Andrew's house. "Where does he live?" Without thinking, Krishna returns to the front office.

"There he is!" the dragon booms out. Out of the corner of his eye, he sees the imposing shape of the Principal coming toward him. As he bolts out the front door, he hears her angry voice echoing through the hallways and off the brick facing of the school: "Don't bother coming back!"

Krishna crosses the street and goes into the shopping mall. Andrew's last name is Richards; he crumples two pages from the telephone book when he sees how many addresses he would have to check. His eyes are desperate and wild.

Large numbers of kids from the school are traversing the mall, playing video games, or seated in the numerous junk food places. Krishna searches, failing to find anyone he knows well enough. He collapses on a bench outside a florist's shop. A young security guard wearing a pale blue blazer tells him to move along. Too numb to be enraged, he absently gets up and notices Roxanne walking alone. With surprising clarity, he feels remorse for abusing her. Her sympathy would be welcome now. Then he has what he assumes to be a stroke of luck. Trish and Charlie are seated together in a doughnut shop next to the florist, talking comfortably over two styrofoam coffees. He starts over as they look up, see him, and look back down into their coffees. Trish is quick to reverse herself, greeting him with a false smile on her face.

"Hi, Kris!"

"Trish, Charlie . . . . " He tries to make a pleasantry about skipping classes but the words stick to his tongue. "I need help," he hears himself say.

"What's the matter?" asks Charlie.

"Do you guys know where Andrew lives?"

A faint smile appears on Charlie's face which he turns into a frown, but not quickly enough.

"You knew! Why didn't you tell me?"

"Sit down, Kris," Trish says. "We'll buy you a coffee."

"Where does he live, you bastards?"

"Tell him to shut his mouth, Trish. That's what's gotten him into trouble in the first place."

The shaking begins again. A remote part of his intellect warns him that he is going to do something violent or break down in tears in front of these two people who now seem to him like strangers.

"There he goes again, the Wacky Paki." How can this person he once loved call him a Paki?

"Shut up, Charlie." Trish, trying to help, gets up from the table and puts her arm around Krishna's shoulders. "Don't do anything stupid, Kris. There's nothing to worry about."

"My name is Krishna, you jerk!" He walks away.

◆

At home, waiting, he sits on the sofa with his face buried in his hands. Krishna, the cause of his sister's undoing. He tries vainly to read a magazine, but is distracted by the image of Najma's innocent face. He walks around the house, slamming doors. Finally, he kneels, promising God and all the spirits of the universe that if everything works out well, he will never drink another drop.

"Prove it! For once, do something!" He grabs a shopping bag, goes into the townhouse garage where the family has a locked fenced-in storage area adjacent to the parking space. He unlocks the fence and the cooler where he keeps an emergency supply of liquor. Four bottles: one Beefeater Gin, one Southern Comfort, two flasks of Seagrams 7. He places the bottles in the shopping bag and carries them out to an empty lot, soon to be a building site, across the street from the townhouse. He finds a small pit, lays each of the precious bottles side by side, picks up a rock and smashes all four.

Three-fifteen, school is out. She would not dare stay out late, knowing that her brother would start asking questions. Where should he confront her? He decides upon the living room, the place where his parents confront him.

He thinks of the night both parents had pleaded with him to help his father again in the store. Krishna refused, telling them he planned to buckle down and spend extra time on his schoolwork in order to go to university. He convinced them and himself that he was turning a new leaf, seeing in his mind the young go-getter wearing a mortarboard, researching and writing an upcoming geography project under the warm lamplight of his desk. His parents, for whom 'university education' was a magic phrase, tried to believe that Krishna was going to change. Remembering their faint smiles of hope, he feels disgusted with himself at having drifted through another term and having today burnt every bridge at the school.

The door opens. Najma. He looks into her frightened eyes. Frightened, but are they still innocent?

"Where have you been?" he asks less with anger than love and concern.

"At school. Why?"

"You weren't in class."

"Are you checking up on me, Krishna? And who looks after you?"

"Where did you go?"

"You tell me."

"I saw you with Andrew Richards when I came to school this morning. Then you didn't go to English class."

Cornered and having little practice with deceit, Najma's face crumples and breaks into tears. "What happened? Tell me what happened, little one."

"He's been so nice to me this week."

Krishna's tone changes to sarcasm. "Did he tell you how beautiful you look? Did he compliment your hair? Did he . . ."

"I felt sorry for him because of the bruise on his face."

"Fool!"

"All right. We did leave school, Krishna. He bought me a Coke. We saw you come into the Mall. We were sitting in front of that place across from the doughnut shop. Trish and Charlie knew we were there, but she didn't want you to start a fight or do something crazy. You looked like you would do something crazy."

Daring to hope, he asks, "Then you went back to school?"

She shakes her head. "We skipped the whole day."

"Where did you go? Where?" He wants to slap her backhanded, as he has seen actors do to women in the movies.

"We went to his house. Please don't tell Father."

Krishna stops breathing, his face suddenly a death mask.

"Nothing happened, Krishna."

"You went to Andrew's house and nothing happened?" As his lungs begin to work, he becomes aware of a sharp pain in his chest.

"What do you want to hear? I told you nothing happened. He was nice to me. We ate from the refrigerator, we talked, we watched television. Then Andrew got up from the couch, looked at me, shook his head and told me I should go home."

"Najma . . . Najma . . . Najma." Exhausted, Krishna hugs her. He forces himself to feel thankful for this one unexpected act of decency. Simultaneously, but more powerfully, he tastes the tears of humiliation.

✧

The bus ride is short from the north of Scarborough where Krishna lives to a computerized driverless aboveground train called the Light Rapid Transit. Even when crowded with commuters, the only sound one ever hears from inside the cars is the hum of the doors opening and closing. Today, Saturday, the train is empty. After five stops, Krishna transfers to the regular subway and then on to another bus to another world, Gerrard Street.

It is almost noon. Spring has finally come. The street is colourful—

much red, white, and gold—and aromatic. People are talking to each other, lingering on the sidewalk and, in the stores, arguing prices and politics in the Punjab.

"Krishna?" His father greets him with outstretched hands and a wide-eyed look of surprise.

"Got something for me to do today, Dad?"

"Of course. Of course." His proud smile forces a grin from Krishna's face.

UNDER THE BRIDGE

STEVEN LIVES IN THE BASEment, preferring the cold and dampness to the physical comfort of his old bedroom adjacent to his parents'. His cot is near the furnace, and two plastic shower curtains hang from the beams to provide an enclosure. A window above the bed looks out into the street from ground level, allowing Steven to see up to the knees of passersby.

Why he has decided to pass the remainder of his teenage years from this peculiar vantage point is a mystery to his parents. They know that beneath the cot is a large old metal tool box. Steven has fixed the lock, removed the rust spots, and repainted the whole thing a bright silver. They do not know that the box now contains memorabilia from the Second World War, iron crosses, SS pins, skull rings, for which he has combed the antique stores of Queen Street. Nor are they aware that underneath the two fold-out drawers of Nazi knick-knacks, sitting alone in metal solitude, is a handgun.

To amuse himself, Steven carefully removes the gun from the box and points it toward the basement window. Lightly fingering the trigger, he waits as a pair of legs appear, gray suit trousers over polished black loafers, skirt bottom with stockings and high heels on their way home from work, or blue jeans over running shoes coming home from school. He closes his eyes and imagines the ultimate, a loud report, the shattering of glass, the legs crumpling to the sidewalk, perhaps a fedora or a baseball cap bouncing away under a parked car.

Little is left of youth in Steven's sixteen-year-old face. He wears his scars proudly. He scowls. His blonde hair is cropped very short and a thin gold ring dangles from his ear. His style of dress completes the picture. He always wears a racist t-shirt, a pair of dark trousers held up by suspenders, and, over it all, a large black raincoat left open to fly in the breeze like a vampire's wings. Originally, the look was cultivated to impress other tough young men.

◆

Angie, a red-haired girl Steven had known only vaguely, asked him to walk with her after school. Soon, he found himself at the apartment of an immense bearded man, Gary, amongst people he wanted to know better. The apartment seemed to be a second home to Gary's young friends, and it was well supplied with beer, food, and uppers. Angie and Steven seated themselves together on a Salvation Army couch and were both handed beers by their smiling, affable host. Angie removed her coat and Steven noticed that she was dressed in her usual way, jean jacket and torn jean shorts over black tights. She moved right next to him and pressed her leg hard against his. The other people in the room, Gary and his friends, kept staring at the two of them. Steven realized suddenly that he was about to be initiated into the group and that the rite would have something to do with this girl.

Angie complained endlessly about a student who was harassing her. She broke into tears and yelled out, "It's about fucking time somebody did something!"

"What'd you say his name was?" asked Gary.

"Earl Taylor."

"Are you scared of this guy, Steven?"

Steven laughed and said, "I see him at school. I'll take care of him."

Angie, in what seemed like long practised moves, took away his beer and put down her own, stubbed out her cigarette, exhaled a stream of smoke, and began to run her hand up and down his inner thigh. "Earl Taylor's as good as dead," Steven said in a trembling voice. He felt trapped and, with no idea what was expected of him, fearful of being exposed as a pretender. Angie reached up and pulled his face down to hers. After a long kiss, she climbed on top of him and reached beneath his shirt, moving her hands up and down his body. Then she removed his raincoat and slid off his suspenders. While the springs of the old couch jabbed into his back and his new-found brothers stared down at him, the panic and the last remnant of youth in his face was evident to everyone. "Let's skip this part for once," Angie said to the others, "I can tell you he's okay." In this way, she had saved them both from having to undress in front of everyone. Gary then escorted the two of them into his bedroom, walked out, and closed the door.

Steven would never stop thinking about what happened in that bedroom. After Angie removed her clothes, whatever desire he still felt ebbed away. Was it the pungent odour? The large triangle of hair? The row of suicide scars along both wrists? Angie soothed him, rubbing his back and shoulders, saying over and over, "You're good. You're good, Steven." In a normal situation, he might have reached out to her as well, but he knew that the others waiting outside the door were expecting something more of him.

An idea came to him as natural as breathing. He asked her to put her clothes back on and she complied. Then he tore the clothes off her body piece by piece, took her down and held her on the floor. She resisted, but just enough for a struggle; the struggle aroused him. Yes, he thought, this was his moment to join the world of men. More powerful and alive than he had ever felt with any girl before, he entered her. Suddenly, like a sea anemone, she trapped him with her insides. He was being drawn down, extended, by rings of muscle. How could this be? Gripped, pulled ever further into her vortex, his throat began to close. He felt intense pleasure, akin to annihilation. Then fear. He recalled the horror of being at the mercy of an older boy at camp who was holding his head under water. He was afraid now, as he had been then, of losing himself. Gasping in desperation and drawing on every bit of strength he could muster, he pulled himself out with a cry, exploding on to the sheet. He knew that he had failed. He could not explain it to her, why he had been unable to go on, this fear he felt. So he said to her instead, "You're so damned ugly!" This taunt she was only too ready to believe. She turned away from him.

"Gary's rule. He has to make sure you're not gay," a tall spectral young man named Wes later told him. "It's real important to him. You can't be gay."

Gary, overhearing, put his arm around Steven and laughed. "Don't listen to him. I got nothing against gay people. I believe in their right to choose . . . between a rope and the electric chair."

A hard metal object was placed in Steven's hand. He looked down and saw a gun. Again, his face betrayed uneasiness. "Have a drink, Steven." Laughing, Gary handed him a white bowl filled with red wine, except the heaviness and the knobbly rock-like feel of it made Steven realize it was not a bowl at all. He drank and then held the object at arm's length. It was a human skull, its apertures sealed with Plaster of Paris.

❖

Steven's father has to keep telling himself that those clothes, that scowl, that attitude are just a phase. He thinks the less said about these things the better, that undue attention exacerbates the problem. Still, the tool box beneath the bed nags at him. His son has never shown an inclination to build anything. Mr. Walling has tried but failed to get inside.

Every morning, father and mother sit together eating breakfast and discussing Steven at the kitchen table. Like many parents, they rebuke themselves for not having spent more time with their son, for pursuing careers, for involving themselves with political causes while the child grows further and further away. Surely, though, there is still time to turn things around. But every time they try to talk to him about his poor grades at school, the blood on his clothing, or the marks on his face, they are answered by silence. He comes up from his basement, eats next to nothing, and quickly disappears.

❖

His parents did not understand. Nothing they could say would change the fact that Steven just plain enjoyed the feeling of being in a fight. He liked throwing punches, knees, kicks to the face, drawing back, seeing the blood and the damage and coming back together to inflict even greater pain and deeper wounds. He loved as well the moment when his wasted opponent finally gave in to his superior power. It was a need more fundamental to him than food. He never questioned any of it, just lived his life according to his feelings. Like a gunfighter or knight-errant waiting to take on the next challenge, there were more than enough angry kids for him in any school or on any street corner in Toronto. Gary and his friends understood.

He proved himself many times, goading fellow students or pretending to be incensed by a remark that had supposedly been said about him. In order to avoid school authorities, all of the resulting fights took place in a park down the street. The ritual was always the same, moving from provocation to challenge to trysting place. However, Earl Taylor, the boy he was supposed to beat up for Angie, refused to meet him at the park, so he broke his head open on a locker in the gym change room.

The incident caused him to be banished from his gym class to the library under the eye of the librarian, Mr. Farnham. At first, Steven tried to intimidate the man by staring, but Larry Farnham smiled back. He liked the challenge of saving wayward students, and the gym teacher who hated Steven was only too ready to oblige him.

Boredom soon induced Steven to wander through the stacks where he settled upon a large section of Second World War books. Subsequently, he spent his time leafing through glossy photos of Nazi officers, goose-stepping soldiers, and the victims of their ideology, staring back, gaunt and skeletal, or piled in fields, or lining the bottoms of mass graves. Larry, walking by one afternoon and noticing the absorbed and smiling face looking at the pictures, asked Steven what he found so fascinating.

"You see those people?" Steven asked, pointing to a photograph of a city square filled with dark-suited Jews, their wives and children, hands held high over their heads. "They did them a favour by killing them."

"Why would you say a thing like that?"

"They're fucking pitiful!" As he spoke, Steven kicked the table leg very hard. The anger was so sudden that Larry jumped back involuntarily. "I hate people who give up without a fight."

"What would you do in the face of a gun, Steven?"

"Nobody lives forever, man."

Close up, Larry noticed beneath the boy's open raincoat a white t-shirt emblazoned with a black cross inside a black circle.

"What's that supposed to mean?" Larry asked, pointing to the symbol.

"White pride."

"You really are something, aren't you?"

"I'm proud of who I am, not like the rest of you bleeding hearts."

❖

Angie. She has marked him like an animal. Often his body re-experiences the moment of pleasure before the panic. This tangible memory gnaws at him, draws him to her in the hallways. He bumps against her at her locker, finding even her smell alluring now. He tells her he is sorry for what he said. He is not sure if her smile means forgiveness.

Standing over her, he plays the scene over and over in his mind, tells himself that all he needs is one more chance. Next time he's going to show her. Fasten on to her like an octopus. Keep himself inside her until she drops open and her hold upon him gives way. Take her will. "I gotta go to class," she says, pushing him gently aside and giving him a little kiss on the ear. Does she know his thoughts?

❖

Gary stretches out on Steven's cot while Wes sits with Steven on the cold basement floor. They have come uninvited for a visit. Steven has been told by others in the group to expect this visit, that one day they will come by surprise and take him with them. He has never been told what they will ask him to do.

Although his mother said nothing to her son, she is appalled that the giant bearded man and the anorexic boy with the shaved head are his friends. In the living room above the three young men, Mr. Walling talks to her. "I don't know any more than you do about them."

"Maybe it's time to move out of the city, Paul."

Below, Gary unwraps three small white pills from a piece of tinfoil, swallows one himself, gives one to Steven, and the other to Wes. Steven pulls out the tool box and displays his collection. With reverence, the two visitors fondle each item and allow the light to reflect off their polished surfaces. Gary holds up a small silver pin, the letters SS.

"I want this," he says. "Okay if I take it?" Without waiting for an answer, Gary sticks the pin on the collar of his leather jacket.

"Why not? Sure." Wes and Gary say something but Steven loses the thread. He hears his own voice speaking. "Be my guest, man." What was that pill he swallowed? "How long have you guys known what's-her-name? . . . Angie?"

Gary laughs. The question has caught all three of them by surprise. "You got a prom coming up at school?"

"Just curious," Steven says.

"Told you he's got the itch," Gary says to Wes. "You like her, Steven?"

"You kidding?" Steven says this in such a way that his desire for her is transparent.

"Tell you what, Steven, we know you like her. We'll get you set up later. Come with us to the ravine."

"Ravine?" What does this have to do with Angie? Steven starts laughing as if he is being tickled.

"Take your gun. Just in case. You never know when we might need it." Steven waits until he sees that Gary is serious, pulls the gun from the tool box and slides it into the inner pocket of his raincoat. The walk up the basement stairs seems to take forever. Leading the other two, he steps into the living room. To his parents, he says, "We're going out."

His father tries to talk. He sees no reason not to ask the questions any father would ask.

"Where you fellows going?"

"Out," Steven says.

"No fooling." Mr. Walling laughs. Then, looking directly at Gary and Wes, he says, "I didn't catch your names." He notices the SS pin on Gary's collar. "They can talk, can't they, Stevie?"

"Shut up, Dad," Steven says.

Mockery. Mr. Walling knows he has made a mistake. He should have tried to talk with his son alone. Steven and his two friends walk out the front door. "I couldn't stop him from leaving, could I?" he asks his wife.

◆

Bored with the Nazi photos, Steven took to hanging around Larry's circulation desk. Sometimes he might talk to him about a piece of news that happened to be on the radio that morning—a rape, an abduction, accident, bombing, or mass murder. At first, Larry forced himself to believe that Steven was trying to make contact with him in the only way he knew. He even gave him the job of handling book loans. However, the sight of the crop-haired boy in the black raincoat had begun to give him a queasy feeling. True, he had offered to deal with difficult students, even if Steven Walling was not quite what he'd had in mind. Larry believed that vulnerability, openness, and optimism could never be completely absent in the young, and no matter how abused and hurt a child might be, he could find some small store of goodness left inside the heart.

One morning, during a slow period, Larry pushed a returned book across to him. "I thought you might be interested in this . . . for a change."

"Is this bleeding heart stuff?" Steven asked. He stood there smiling and shaking his head.

"Give it a try, Steven."

Steven pushed the book back to Larry.

"Just take it home and see if you have the odd moment," the librarian said. "You can bring it back when you want."

Steven hesitated, considered, then deliberately dropped the book on to the carpet. The thought of Gary, Wes, Angie, and the others made him feel invincible. "Don't give me bleeding heart stuff," he said as he got up and stomped off.

Larry watched him leave, wondering whether Steven would return tomorrow and start up as if nothing had happened.

◇

The November wind seems milder down in the ravine. Is it the pill he took that makes it feel like early September? In the twilight, the three of them hike through bright mounds of wet fallen leaves. Passing by the huge overpass with the subway running through its belly, they stop underneath a narrow footbridge. Wes and Steven squat down while Gary sits just below the far end of the bridge. They listen in the growing darkness to the sound of footsteps on the wooden slats. Occasionally, Gary peeks through an opening in the bushes to see who is coming. Three times he looks down at them and shakes his head. Suddenly, Gary's body tenses like a cat at a mouse hole. "Yeah, this guy." He nods to Wes and swings up on to his end of the bridge.

Quickly, Wes takes Steven to the opposite end. As Steven comes up on to the bridge, a man comes toward the two of them. Gary is now walking slowly behind the man, who has turned around to avoid Gary's large and fearsome figure. Surrounded, his eyes pick out Steven and stare in a silent gesture of appeal. Wes steps forward, and as the man freezes in panic, Gary lifts him up from behind and throws him over the bridge railing three meters down into the mass of leaves. Steven vaults down after him and grabs the stunned victim by the jacket, hurling him down again. He is exhilarated. As Gary and Wes come over to watch, Steven slams a punch into his rib cage and kneels down on top of him. The man, covered almost entirely by Steven's raincoat, struggles to free himself, then suddenly stops.

Matter-of-factly, Gary says, "Kill the faggot."

Steven laughs. "I'd like to," he says, certain that Gary is only trying to scare the guy.

"He said to kill it," says Wes very softly, and this time Steven knows that the request is anything but a joke.

"Faggot. Fucking queer bastard!" Steven yells, taking the gun from his raincoat and bringing the short barrel to the man's lips. "Open your fucking mouth!" The man's eyes stare at him. "I said open up!" The mouth opens. The gun barrel goes in. The man's eyes are filled with fear. Steven thinks he recognizes those eyes in the ever dimming light.

His face distorted by a frozen smile, Steven looks up at Gary and Wes, hoping for a reprieve.

"Whatsa' matter, Steven?" Gary asks.

No, it won't work; no matter how angry he tries to be, he cannot pull the trigger. He pulls the gun from the man's mouth and starts to beat him about the head with it. The man screams for help with what little strength he has left.

Steven leans back as something heavy suddenly comes down on the nose, on the forehead, with huge thuds. The eyes are covered with blood. "You don't use a gun on this shit. You kill it like a cockroach," Gary says, tossing aside the heavy stone.

A voice comes from the bridge overhead. "Hey, what're you doing?" The three look up in unison to see the top of a head disappear. They hear footsteps running off.

"For chrissake, get off," Wes whispers to Steven, having to pull him off the now inert body. The three trot into the cover of oncoming darkness.

◆

On the subway, Steven tries to talk about it. "Did I do all right?" he asks. There are a few people in the car so Gary and Wes tell him to shut up. They are worried, but they think that it had probably been too dark for anyone to see them clearly. In vain, Steven keeps searching their faces for reassurance. Gary suddenly looks alarmed and whispers, "Close your raincoat, asshole." Steven looks down to see the wash of blood on his t-shirt.

◆

Back at Gary's apartment, while Gary and Wes appear calm, Steven's body starts to tremble. He can barely hold his beer in his hand. Rock music bursts like machine gun fire from two large speakers.

He does not know how long he has waited, staring at the door, when she finally arrives. She's with a tall thin goateed man in stovepipe jeans they call The Stork. Steven, overwhelmed by need and feeling that he has earned her, walks up to Angie, disregarding Stork. "Dance?" he half requests, half commands.

"Tell little boy, here, to bugger off," Angie says loudly to Stork.

"Just a fucking minute!" Steven says, grabbing her arm and holding it behind her back. Stork and Gary grab him. He breaks free momentarily, but is recaptured and held against the wall by the lapels of his raincoat, a knee poised at his groin. A cry escapes him.

Angie comes over and grabs Stork around his narrow waist, putting her hand deep into the front pocket of his jeans. Then she says, "You can have me, Stevie. One day when you're not too scared to lose your rubber dickie." Laughing, she takes Stork with her into Gary's bedroom.

◆

Home. He must have shot out of Gary's apartment and come all the way home with his eyes shut. He cannot remember how he got into the basement.

"Steven, telephone."

His father's voice momentarily scares him. He comes upstairs and takes the call in his father's study. "Yeah?"

"You alone?" a voice asks.

He looks behind him. His father has remained in the hallway. "Yeah."

"It's Angie. Don't hang up. They picked up Gary." She pauses. "Got someplace you can go?"

Steven does not answer.

"Steven, I'm sorry. I was mad at you. I'll help you get away."

He hangs up the phone. His head feels top-heavy, his body hollow, as if his entire being has elevated into his brain.

"Steven." His father comes into the study. "Who was that on the phone?"

"I don't know . . . friend," he slurs. Slowly, his head rocks back and forth.

"Girlfriend, huh? You never told me you had a girlfriend. Hey, what's wrong? Sit down for a second. I want to talk to you." Steven sits down on the love seat opposite his father's desk. "I don't think we've had a talk in a long time, have we?" Mr. Walling sits beside his son, and puts a fatherly arm around his shoulders.

"No."

"Look at me, Stevie. What can I do? I'm worried about you, what you're turning into. Come on, what's happening with you? Can't we talk about it?"

For the moment, Steven is too dazed to listen. He stares at the desk.

His father continues. "Is it because you think we didn't want you? Maybe you overheard us arguing the day I told your mother that you came along at the wrong time. Well, that's not true. People say all kinds of things they don't mean. We make mistakes. We're human. I . . . we just wanted you to know that we think you're a good person."

Steven only hears the last sentence. His head stops rocking. "Would you say that if you knew I just killed someone?"

"What? . . . "

Turning around to face his father, he asks, pleading to be heard, "What if I killed somebody? What would you do?"

"That's sick, talking like that. I'm just trying to tell you that I love you." With that, his father tries to embrace him fully, but Steven holds out his hand and turns aside. "It's okay for me to hug you, isn't it?"

"His eyes were all blood, Dad. I couldn't stop staring at it. Blood all over. Look!" Steven turns back and opens his raincoat. His father gapes, then covers his face. Wanting to explain, Steven opens his mouth. Instead, he gets to his feet and starts to retch, then throws up all over the love seat and the area rug. Despite it all, his father remains frozen in place. Steven walks away with a heavy shuffle.

◆

The gun. Finger on the trigger, he points the gun out the basement window. Legs appear in the lamplight. He aims. The gun, like a planchette on a Ouija board, slowly begins to move. It turns to face him. Now the tears come . . . . Now.

PAST LIFE

ALIGHTING FROM THE STREET-car, Peter smiled to himself as he considered his recent accomplishments: a job, a girlfriend, a place of his own. All right, a joe-job, a girlfriend who made him jealous with her other commitments, a windowless room in a Scarborough basement that ate up most of his piddling salary. Still, he had taken a step beyond life in a group home, and this after so many people had said he would never amount to anything.

He walked, as one sometimes does, unconscious of his destination, but the neighbourhood began to look familiar. The house on the corner of the dead end street, which he had thought of as large and formidable, now seemed just a red brick box with two floors. An old couple used to wave to him from the veranda. This day the weather was warm, but no one was sitting outside to welcome him. Various children's toys, most noticeably a front-end loader and a remote control truck, were strewn haphazardly along with a baby stroller across the porch.

Mrs. Camp, a divorced actress, her daughter Jill, and Jill's little brother Jody used to live across the street in the house with beautiful brickwork. Flanked by two high rows of hedges at the front was a trellis which gave a glimpse of an elaborate shrub and flower garden behind. For most of his life in the neighbourhood, Peter had played with Jill and Jody, sneaking upstairs every so often to see the beautiful Mrs. Camp rehearsing one of her dinner theatre parts in the cool shadows of her bedroom. She believed at the time that the boy with the soulful eyes had discovered a latent love for the stage. Since the house had changed so little in five years, Peter was certain she must still be there.

He walked east three more houses and stopped in front of his old next door neighbours' place. Of his neighbours, Mike and Sarah, Peter's parents used to say "They live together," with a tone of disapproval. Nonetheless, Peter had been a frequent visitor. Mike had liked his privacy and had often shown impatience at Peter's intrusions. Although Peter could sense this mood when Mike stiffened, he could never resist the impulse to stay and talk. His partner had always been easier to talk to. Sarah had seemed interested in what Peter was doing and remembered to ask about things he told her the last time. Mike would then say something in a tone of voice that would indicate he was trying to end the conversation, like "Well, Pete," or "Anyways," and he would clap his hands and rub them together as if he were Johnny Carson about to introduce the next guest. But Sarah would just keep on talking. Then Mike would look at his watch. Actually, Peter liked them both very much. On his good days, Mike had a sense of humour, and had once even wrestled with Peter in the garden.

Peter climbed the porch stairs, noticing that the wood under the straw matting was spongy and that the grey paint at the sides had chipped away to reveal a red undercoating. He stared into the bay window and saw a shadow walking by at the rear. He banged on the heavy wooden door and hurt his hand. He had forgotten how that door could hurt his hand. He waited. He knocked again, lighter this time.

The door opened. It was Mike in his checkered bathrobe. He had the same dark, bushy eyebrows, but in five years his hair and moustache and shaggy beard had gone from black to salt and pepper, and he looked smaller. Pieces of his breakfast sat in his beard.

"Yeah?"

"I wondered if you'd be interested in a subscription to *The Star*?"

He pointed to the blue box on the front porch which was already overflowing with *Toronto Stars*. "You think we need two copies? Wait. Don't I know you? . . . Pete!" Then, turning around, "Sarah, it's Petey-boy! Back from the dead. How've you been? I didn't recognize you. You must have grown or something."

"Yeah? How do I look?"

"Great!" Something in Mike's tone of voice lead Peter to believe that he didn't mean it. Moreover, Peter was still small and acutely conscious of the fact. "You're not really selling subscriptions, are you?"

"No."

"Same old Pete," he said to Sarah, also in her bathrobe and looking a great deal larger than Peter remembered.

"So, I look good, huh?"

"Sure you do. Doesn't he?" Mike asked her.

"Why don't you invite him in, Mike?"

"What's this for?" Mike put a finger on the first in a row of four gold rings descending from the top of Peter's ear.

"You like 'em?"

"It's okay."

"I think they're great!" said Sarah. "They make you look tough—like a pirate. Come on in."

Stepping inside, noticing the chaos—sections of the Saturday newspaper strewn over the couch and on the dark wooden floors, egg-stained plates, spoons, half-empty cups—Peter breathed in the familiarity, the smells of strong spices, coffee, toast, and a smell that he did not remember, like a scented powder.

"Would you guys have anything to eat? Look, I don't want to put you to any trouble or anything . . . ."

Mike rolled his eyes, but Sarah, without hesitation, went to find him something.

"Haven't they fed you next door?" Mike asked.

"I haven't been over there yet."

"Really?"

Peter was finally forced to ask himself what he was doing there. Finding no reasonable answer, he could not stop his body from moving. As Mike looked on, stunned by Peter's audacity but also amused by his discomfiture, Peter examined a Visa bill, whistled at the total, and put it back down on the coffee table. He turned over a black glass ashtray shaped like a mutated scallop and examined the bottom, noting that it was from Mexico. He took one of the half-dozen Indian masks off the wall and tore off the hook trying to replace it.

"Sorry," Peter said.

"Just leave it there," Mike said icily.

A large bookcase provided a temporary focus; it seemed impossible that two people could have read so much. He leafed through a stack of books sitting on a board above the radiator—Piaget, Spock, Brazelton, volumes on baby care, breastfeeding, child-rearing. He turned a lamp on and off. Passing by the coffee table again, he noticed a gold ring on the floor underneath. He was hoping to be rescued, to hear Sarah's voice inviting him to sit down to breakfast.

"What have you been up to, buddy?"

Peter smiled and gave what he thought must sound like a knowing laugh. He saw an Indonesian gong hanging by a thick string from a doorknob. Feeling Mike's eyes burning into his skin, he picked up the striker. He gave the gong an enormous thwack.

"No!"

Suddenly, the cry of a baby rang out from an invisible monitor.

"Shit! We just put him down." Mike frowned. "It wouldn't be so bad but he was up all night with the colic. I had to walk the floors with him."

Sarah, coming in, glared at Peter as she spoke to her husband. "Mike, finish the breakfast stuff I started for Pete." She went upstairs to care for the howling child, who would have been perfectly audible without the monitor which Peter now spotted at the stairway window.

The young man, amazed, could only point up the stairs and ask, "When?"

"Two months old, sixty days, and I haven't slept since he came home from the hospital."

"Boy?"

Mike nodded.

"What's his name?"

"Nelson."

"Nelson?"

"After Nelson Mandela. You don't like it, eh? Maybe you're right. So far, it's been like a South African prison around here. At least six times a night, the lights are shining."

"He's had a shit!" Sarah shouted down.

"That's probably the whole thing, right there. He needed a shit."

Peter felt relieved, now thinking perhaps he had done well to hit the gong. Then Mike began to laugh. "It's all we ever talk about anymore: shit, piss, vomit . . . and the colours thereof. Can you believe we'd ever do this?"

Peter followed Mike into the kitchen, but not before retrieving the gold ring from under the coffee table and pocketing it.

"You still haven't told me what you're doing with yourself," Mike said, buttering a piece of burnt toast.

"Working."

"No kidding? At what? Like some coffee? Kona. Best goddamned coffee in the world. Grown on volcanoes or something."

"I manage a record store."

"Manage? Pretty good!"

"I make between thirty-five and forty," he lied.

"Already? Milk?" Mike poured some milk from a pitcher into the coffee.

"Would you happen to have some sugar?"

"Jesus! I'll ask Sarah." As if on cue, she entered cradling Nelson wrapped in a baby blanket.

"Where do we keep the sugar, dear? Peter wants to ruin this perfectly good cup of coffee."

She reached into the back of the pantry and pulled out an unopened Domino Sugar box. Peter took it as she turned, pushed in the perforated flap, and guiltily poured a generous amount into his cup.

Drinking rapidly and stuffing the toast into his mouth, his need to move around became even more pronounced. He fingered the ring in his pocket.

"Pete's got a job managing a record store."

"Oh, where?"

"Queen Street," Peter said, looking at Nelson, poking a finger in the baby's red blotchy face. "He's cute." A group home worker had told him that flattery, especially flattery of people's children, would get them to like him. The gesture did nothing more than set off a fresh round of howls. Nelson turned a dark purple.

"What the hell's the matter with him now?" asked Mike.

"He's still not used to strangers." The blanket unravelled with the baby's wild kicking.

"I think he's a goddamned manipulator, if you want to know," said Mike.

"And you're a goddamned idiot," his partner replied, as she took Nelson back upstairs.

Looking at the stairs but talking to Peter, Mike muttered, "The little bastard's gonna get the teat again." After a pause, he said, "Damn, you're lucky, you know. I'd do just about anything to get my freedom back. Where you living?"

"Just got my own place." Peter smiled at the thought of his windowless cell in Scarborough.

"I'll bet you did. Getting any action?"

"My share, I guess."

"Goddamn, you always did have a sweet tooth." Mike pointed with his thumb across the street. "Whatever happened between you and her?"

Peter smirked.

"Damn, you're lucky. You've always been lucky," reiterated the older man.

"I don't know."

"Guys like you—it falls in your lap."

He was astonished and disappointed at the same time to realize that Mike was jealous of him. "Mike, what could be better than this? You've got a house, a child, a wife who loves you . . . "

"Shut up."

"What else could you want?!"

"I told you—it's a prison." Mike looked at his watch. "Anyways, Pete, I've got stuff to do this morning. Why don't you drop in next door? I'm sure they'd love to see you."

"Sure, buddy." Nothing new. His visits always ended that way; either he would say or do something to cause annoyance.

Instead of turning to his old home, his eyes again fixed on the Camp house, her house. "Whatever happened between you and her?" Mike's question forced a memory, still palpable, into his consciousness:

Mr. BMW tools into her driveway, emerges smoothly from the car in his brown leather jacket which makes him seem a part of the upholstery, and rings her doorbell. She comes out the door in her calf-length black wool skirt and tight red sweater accentuating her nipples, and he escorts her to the car, his hand on her bum. She arches back her long neck and kisses him over her shoulder, a long deep kiss, absently waving goodbye to Jill and

Jody and the babysitter. He helps her into the car, never once removing his hand from her bum until he steps back to close the door.

Unknown to her, he had been her slave, overbrimming with desire, an insatiable, erotic pubescent. Summer nights, trespassing inside the hedges of her front yard, he had stared at her shadow through the Venetian blinds, stared as he stood near the flowerbeds, rose up like a tropism, pulled down his shorts and ejaculated into the ripe leaves of a forsythia and on to the soil beneath his feet.

Even now, as Peter had done so many times before, he imagined his own hand moving smoothly up and down that black wool, the curve of that bum, the points of those breasts, and Mrs. Camp nuzzling up to his lips, purring.

Closing his eyes as tightly as he could, he tore himself from the spot. He walked over to his old home, gathered up his resolve and rang the doorbell which played the same familiar song of his childhood: 'Big bells do chime.' He could never hear those four notes without remembering the words. The door opened and there stood his mother—Mother—what she insisted he call her despite her reserve. Mrs. Paley.

"Peter."

"Hi, thought I'd drop by to say hello."

"Come in, Peter."

"Everything looks just the same around here."

She ushered him into the living room where the man who was once his father, his mouth twisted off to the side, sat in front of a TV set which played soundlessly. "Dad, Peter's come to visit." The man nodded but remained mute. "Dad's had his stroke, you know. He can't speak anymore, but he gets around just fine."

Seeing his father in this condition made him anxious again. He dearly wished he hadn't come.

Mrs. Paley went on. "I suppose some things are the same, as you say, but a lot has changed. Your brother is in the last year at university and your sister has graduated and gotten a managerial position with Zellers. We always said Peter could have done the same, didn't we, Dad?" Mr. Paley nodded sadly. "And of course you've changed, haven't you? We received your letter . . . "

"Not changed really. Just went back to who I was before."

"Peter Blanchette. Yes, although I can't understand why you'd want..."

"Mother..."

"... the name of some Frenchman who knew the walls of two penitentiaries."

"He's my father."

With surprising vehemence, she said, "Peter, stop pretending!" And then, pointing to her husband, "Is this not your real father?"

"You don't understand. I didn't deserve any more from you than what I got. I just came by to say thank-you. I had to leave here so fast I never had a chance to say thank-you for all you did." Peter was not sure whether he meant it, but his statement momentarily quieted Mrs. Paley. The couple stared at him in wonderment. "Mind if I see my old room?"

Mrs. Paley duly lead him up the stairs. "We'll be leaving here soon, Peter, so we've gotten rid of a lot of things." Indeed, only his bed and desk remained. His posters were gone, as were the TV with the channel changer, the stereo, the computer, the private telephone, the sea of possessions which exceeded anything his brother or sister ever had. Peter felt his throat tighten.

Mrs. Paley began to talk again. "We tried, Peter. We so wanted everything to work out. But after you—we just knew you needed the kind of help we couldn't give."

"I know I was a handful," Peter said, descending the stairs, tears in his voice. He was surprised at himself for not turning around to say what he truly felt: "Why'd you give up on me? If only you'd stuck it out!"

Back in the street, he walked very slowly, hoping to find out if Mrs. Camp still lived there. Even after five years, her house had maintained its aura for him. The place was quiet with anticipation, just as it appeared years ago on that unforgettable Saturday night.

Peter sneaks across the street, goes around to the back and unhooks the outer window of the basement. He pushes the inner window in, just as he'd seen her housepainter do, and lets himself down into a laundry tub. The door leading from the basement to the kitchen is unlocked. He walks upstairs into her bedroom. He removes his running shoes and all of his clothes and climbs into her bed. The soft cool sheets smell almondy. A silk nightgown smelling of musk is under the pillow. He takes it in his hands, feels its perfection, and wraps it around himself. The room grows dark except for a streetlight shining through the blinds. He waits, trembling, thinking he ought to leave, but the longer he stays, the more he becomes acclimatised to the comfort of her big bed.

Lights move across the wall telling him a car has turned into the driveway. He hears the kids arguing as they walk up to the front porch, hears the garage door come down, and Mrs. Camp unlocking the front door. Jill and Jody exchange insults, go up to their separate bedrooms, and slam the doors. Sighing, Mrs. Camp comes into the room, goes over to the window in the dark, and stares out at the street through the blinds. She reaches down behind her and flicks on the lamp on the night table. Turning around, she sees his face on the pillow, gasps, and then stops perfectly still. Her eyes wander to the floor where Peter's clothes, inside-out jeans, underwear, t-shirt, running shoes, are piled. She stares at him for seconds, minutes, her smooth red face with short golden hairs glistening in the lamplight, her large dark eyes, her lips curled up in a little quizzical smile. And then, fully clothed, she shuts off the lamp and joins him beneath the sheet.

"Poor boy, poor boy," she whispers over and over as she strokes his hair and kisses his face. Peter tries to hold her in his arms but can only encompass half this rich world. Every aspect of her womanhood is fully developed, hips, shoulders, the breasts covered with a soft cotton shirt where he, shuddering, weeping, buries his head, and she holds him for a time so sweet that time no longer matters.

Only later did he discover he had been there for two hours. She had tried to rouse him from his trance-like state, had helped him with his clothes as if he were a toddler, and led him down the stairs. "How did you get in?" she had whispered.

"Basement window."

Mrs. Camp had nodded, walked him through the kitchen, and ever so slowly and quietly let him out the back door.

Mike, sitting on his porch drinking a beer, had seen him coming down the driveway. "Pete, your parents called! Where've you been?"

He had given a foolish wave and walked diagonally across the street to avoid conversation. What could he possibly have said to the guy? Instead, he had left Mike to draw his own conclusions.

How his mother had fretted! How his brother and sister had questioned him! Had he been kidnapped? Run away? The police had been called. Peter had told them that he'd been walking and without realizing had gone too far. No one had believed him, so he bit back angrily, complaining that his family watched over him like jailers. The Paleys had stared at each other, not knowing how to respond to this suddenly alien thirteen-year-old. Mr. Paley, a gentle man, had broken off the questioning and offered him something to eat. Peter had refused, running to his room, where he shut the door and tried to recall the feel and smell of Mrs. Camp, and began to plan how he might be with her again and what further pleasures he might take.

He must have heard the ring of the telephone, but he had been so wrapped up in his thoughts that its possible importance failed to register in his mind. Shortly afterward, he had heard a knock.

"Peter, I want to talk to you," his father had said from outside the bedroom door. Peter had opened the door and bowed his head. "Tell me the truth, now. Where have you been?"

"I took a walk, Dad."

"Don't lie to me, Peter. Why did you break in across the street?"

"Why do you ask if you already know?"

"Don't we give you everything you need?"

It was a question he had heard many times before and which he had never attempted to answer. As for Mrs. Camp, he had not accused her of betrayal because evidently she had not told the whole truth. However, he had known without being told that he had lost the right to enter her house again.

Nonetheless, one afternoon, with the family in the back yard and Mr. BMW playing surrogate daddy at the barbecue, Peter had walked right in the front door and down the hall into the bathroom. The face he had seen in the mirror had not been his own but something strange, wolfish. He had opened the medicine cabinet, removed an unused tube of toothpaste, and squeezed it into the sink in neat spiral rings. From in front of the house where he now waited, he had heard the squeak of the back screen door, her flip-flops walking to the bathroom, a pause of discovery, a loud summons and an interrogation followed by a series of stone-hard slaps to Jody's face. "I didn't do it! I didn't do it!" Jody had protested. Peter recalled having run off to keep his own laughter from being overheard.

A dog turd on her front steps, torn out flowers and shrubs, Jody beaten up at school because of a malicious rumour, all the effects of these further acts he had had the satisfaction of witnessing, but eventually all of the blame had been laid at his feet by his despairing parents, his embarrassed siblings, and an angry neighbourhood. The warnings had been clear: "We don't know what to do with you. Maybe you're unhappy here?"

As Peter stared across the street, he reached into his pocket and felt the ring. A thin gold band. What could have possessed him to steal it? A thought began to form in his mind, a thought that reached the level of feeling but could only be translated as "I want . . . I want." It was as far as he had ever come in trying to articulate the force which drove him.

The final scene had occurred during a late summer heat wave with Jill and Jody away. Mrs. Camp had been weeding and repairing the damage Peter had caused in the garden.

Doesn't she know he is watching her? Of course. Why else has she worn those white shorts with the halter top? Mr. BMW (wouldn't you know it!) drives up and offers her a hand at gardening. A hand, you bet! That hand on that bum, what is she, a goddamned horse? They walk together through the trellis, disappearing behind the hedge, and when she reappears her face is flushed with excitement. He takes her inside, doubtless for a fling, a hop in the hay, before Jill and Jody return home. Too much.

Peter grabs a screwdriver from his basement and runs across the street. Then he scrapes a line around the BMW, then another, and another. Just as he notices the driver's door is unlocked, as he readies himself to puncture the leather upholstery, a hand abruptly turns him around and a fist grazes his left cheekbone. Mr. BMW's rage has thrown off his aim, but the fact that a grown man has tried to attack him causes Peter to cry like a baby.

She must have taken his side because he could still remember Mr. BMW repeating, "I lost it. I lost it." She must have tried to intervene on his behalf when the family had finally decided that Peter Paley, as he was then known, had lost his place in their lives. She must have wept for weeks after he had been sent to the group home.

✧

From her front door, preceded by a movement in the glass, a very tall young man emerged wearing a numbered jersey and a loose fitting pair of shorts, a basketball cradled in his arm. With his tanned features and sleek dark hair, he appeared confident and athletic. Momentarily, he fixed Peter with a stare, then started to walk away, bouncing the ball.

"Jody?" The young man stopped and turned. Peter crossed the street and held out his hand. "How are you, man?"

Jody, a full head taller than Peter, stared as he would at a cockroach. He took the ball, held it in front of him, and snapped his wrists in a rapid motion that caused Peter to flinch. Still holding the ball, he turned and walked off.

"Yeah, fuck you too," Peter mumbled to himself. "Fuck all of you." Nothing else, just the snap of that ball, finally made him relinquish the dream that Jody's mother still loved him, had ever loved him. He quickly left the dead end street and made his way to the streetcar, the subway, the long ride home. At the Pape station, he once again fingered the ring in his pocket. What could he do with it and not compromise himself even further? Give it to his girlfriend who would know he had stolen it? Keep it? They were sure to investigate him, search his room as had happened so many humiliating times at the group home. This time he would face a criminal record. It was, as well, impossible for him to return it, having Mike and Sarah see that he hadn't really changed. Nor was he mercenary enough to sell or pawn it.

The train clattered east into Scarborough. End of the line. As the handful of other passengers escalated into the light, Peter thought hard about the quick death offered by a leap from the platform into the next oncoming train. It would make the six o'clock news. A moment of excruciating pain ... then nothing? The fires of Hell? Or perhaps a new life from which to choose, new parents? If only he could be sure, he would gladly give up this life to be able to say, "Mommy ... Daddy" and to know those words were true. There, he had said it, finally. What a suck he was! As he heard the wheels scream and the blare of the whistle, he tossed the ring to the speeding train to devour.

FOUR I LOVE WITH ALL MY HEART, FIVE I CAST AWAY

IT STARTS BY HURTING. BUT you keep it there. You keep it there and after a while, you don't know how long, the pain goes away. Burning flesh has a smell you can't describe. You watch as the white stuff oozes up from beneath the blisters. But it's no longer your arm that's burning; it's just some ugly thing you don't care about anymore. Moira and Tom, the night staff, look in on the three of us.

"Idiots," Tom says and walks away.

Then Moira: "What are you doing to yourselves? Think about it."

It's always the way here; they give you a choice to do the right thing and, when you don't, you're supposed to realize that it's you who's got the problem. You can't try to blame it on anyone else.

I'm always the last to pull the cigarette from my arm. That's how you win. I keep it there a little bit extra to show Kevin and Bobby they're still hung up by the pain and being disfigured. For me it doesn't matter anymore. I may even begin to like it soon.

"Are you guys finished?" It's Moira again. "Maybe you might like to try running in front of cars or jumping from the subway platform?" You just stare at her. That's all you need to do. Don't argue. Don't explain. Show them the holes you've burned in your arm and stare. It finally shuts them up. There's just nobody in the world who talks more than a child-care worker.

Kevin, Bobby, and me. Three days before Christmas and we're all that's left here. The other kids are home on visits, pretending to be part of some family that doesn't know them any more. We kind of pretend here, too. We put up a Christmas tree downstairs, and tried to decorate it together. Didn't take five minutes before we were arguing and throwing tinsel around the room. It's not as if every day in a year isn't bad enough, but Christmas, it's absolutely the worst.

Sometimes I feel like getting out of here entirely, running out west or going up north. I've seen the Rockies, and they are beautiful. Lake Louise and that, Banff. Space, deep snow, stars. Stand up on a mountain and take a picture of the sunrise. You're higher than the sun. Not much stuff in Toronto is beautiful.

◆

I'm going to sit on my bed, if you don't mind. You're a shrink, eh? You look like a shrink. You say you came here tonight to try and understand me. That's how shrinks talk. I don't usually talk to shrinks anymore. But I'm going to talk to you because the staff and the school are trying to spread lies about me. I can't stand being blamed for stuff I haven't done. So just as long as I know you're going to set people straight . . . I know how I'm supposed to start. When I was little, right? Mom tried to bring us up and Dad went to the bar. He was also fooling around behind her back with a boarder. Along with her day job, Mom had to work three nights a week and Dad would be laying this chick downstairs in the front room, all the while saying, "Don't worry about it, the kids are asleep." Well, Carla may have been asleep. I just tried to keep out of it. I didn't want my Dad to be against me. I'd just lie there half-dazed behind the couch. One night, Mom came home early, her ulcer was making her sick, and she saw them together. Dad didn't even try to defend himself, and, believe me, he was in no position to. She found me behind the couch and that didn't make her any happier. Sick as she was, she just packed our things and took my sister and me out of the house.

Of course, Mom couldn't afford a decent place for us to live, and there was a big waiting list for government housing. Some of the places we looked at you wouldn't keep your dog in and they weren't exactly cheap. We stayed at the hostel for the first three nights while Mom puked up blood. Then her pride finally broke and she left Carla and me with Aunt Mavis. My aunt yelled. You could tell she took us in because family is supposed to do stuff like that. She'd always be telling us that she'd raised three of her own and how they'd turned out so good and she didn't need to be raising someone else's kids. Her arthritis had slowed her down. Every time she got out of a seat, she'd puff and groan. You'd have thought she was delivering a baby when she made breakfast.

Dad came to Aunt's house really pissed off with Mom; he asked us who we wanted to live with. My sister and I thought anything would be better than Aunt Mavis, so we both went with him. I didn't like it there either; I couldn't stand his girlfriends. Dad had gotten used to wanting me to be in the room when he did it with them. He'd let me drink as much as I wanted so I wouldn't complain. After Mom got herself settled and her health had improved, she came and picked up my sister. She'd found a nice room out on Gerrard Street. I was glad for Carla because she just cried all the time at Dad's, never went to school, never did anything except watch the soaps and cry all day. She graduated high school this past fall; I think she's going to become a nurse or something to help people in need and from what I've seen there's plenty of those to go around.

Living with Dad, I went to school drunk and would fight with anyone. I finally got expelled for punching out a teacher. I was late as usual because Dad's sessions would sometimes go on 'til three in the morning. My teacher used to lock the door so that you couldn't just walk in and interrupt her class. I knew she was also a little hard-of-hearing so I started banging on the door. I didn't know the class was away that day on a field trip so I kept banging and screaming, "Let me in!" That's when this East Indian teacher from the next room came out into the hall and asked me to stop banging, that no one was in the class. I called him a cockroach. He was so polite; he just asked me to accompany him to the office. He put his arm around my shoulders; that's gay. I hit him in the teeth as hard as I could. I had to have three operations on my hand from his contaminated mouth.

After that, Dad didn't want me anymore. I had to go to a foster home. Mom let me visit her on weekends. All the time I was there I'd be on liquor and drugs, mostly uppers. I fought with my Mom's boyfriend. He's the kind of alkie who always tells you he's just had a couple of beers when he really means he's just finished off a mickey and a two-four. Whenever he got drunk, which was any day he wasn't sick, he went after her first. He'd pull her hair, punch her tits, anything. I'd try to get in between. Drugs gave me courage plus I'd learned a little self-defense. At first, I'd have to beat the bastard senseless. Then he got afraid of me. So he just told Mom all kinds of stuff about me, worked his way under her skin. This time it was Mom who told me not to come around anymore. I couldn't get on with my foster family, either; they were always on me about my drugs, my messy room, and my schooling, so I just stayed on the street until they had to send me to this group home.

When the group home sent me to the new school, I thought things were getting better. I met a girl named Wendy, a real good dresser, smart; it was enough just to stand together in front of my locker. You don't believe me, I can see, but it's true. It felt so good standing there together barely touching. We started going out together, meeting places. Her parents own a big house just two blocks away from here so it was easy to see each other. One night, we just forgot about the time. Just like in Cinderella. It was the first warm spring night, when the girls start wearing shorts and halter tops and you feel a little bit like the flowers must feel bursting through the soil. We were sitting together on a park bench, that's all we were doing, I swear it, because we didn't need to do any more than that. Sure, we kissed every so often and those kisses seemed to go on and on, but nothing more than that. Her parents got worried about where she was and went through her stuff to find my phone number. Some worker answered the phone, "Howland House." Well, we hadn't gone out of our way to tell them I lived in a group home, so that was all they had to hear. I guess some girls still listen to their parents when they're told not to go out with a guy anymore.

I'm not bitter about it. Everyone steals from everyone. It's a great big circle. They don't feel any guilt about it and neither do I. I just let it ride. It never used to bother me when someone looked hard at me after I'd done something wrong. That was when I stole for attention. Now I just do it and want to be left alone. Cops start blaming you for every damn thing. Sick charges. Like that crap I'm sure they told you about some kid who cut up the blouses and the crotches of girls' pants in the school change room. They think I did that; it's probably the main reason you're here talking to me. I'm the one they always try to put the blame on. The staff must have told you I'm a sex maniac. I'm really not. It's the girls around here. Good-looking and ugly girls want sex all the time. It's only the middle ones that want a relationship. The good-looking ones always do whatever they want. Ugly girls will do anything you want to get you to love them. The chubby ones, I charge them twenty dollars. I don't have any affection for them or nothing; I just pretend to have a good time. Now they're attached to me. That's what always seems to happen when a girl lets you inside of her. She thinks you've gotta be in love with her. I guess it's a little sad, if you think about it. I try not to. The staff had to move me downstairs, but stuff still goes on.

If Mom came for me now, I'd still go with her. I guess that's always been the truth. But she's married into a new family, new kids; I wouldn't really fit in too well, would I? I remember the night when Mom took Carla out to Gerrard Street. She came here with lots of packages in both arms. At first I thought, 'just a Christmas visit.' Lots of presents. Lots of talk about how much we meant to her. And goodbye 'til next Christmas. But then she started talking to Carla about this little place that she could barely turn around in, that she couldn't put a kitchen table into. I got the message. She might just as well have said how she didn't want me there instead of telling me what a tiny place it was and how lucky I was to be able to live with my Dad. I'd have slept on the floor, in the kitchen, anywhere just so I could be away from him and his girlfriends. The one thing my Dad could do well was screw every night. Goddamn her for leaving me there. Maybe I could've made something out of myself too. It was a small place, yeah, but it wasn't too small for her drunken boyfriend.

She keeps telling me that if I don't get better she won't take me back, but the more she leaves me here the sicker and more perverted I get. That's just bullshit, the stuff about taking me back. Truth is nobody gives a shit about me and neither do I. I have crazy thoughts. It might have been me, you know. The change room. I'm not sure if I dreamt about it because I overheard the story or if I'm really the one who did it. It must've been a dream. I'm walking the halls looking for something. I do that a lot because teachers don't want me in their classes; when I skip they don't bother to check up on me. I see the door to the girls' change room and I just walk in. Clothes, bags, shoes, just lying around waiting for someone to put the life back into them. I'm very good with a switch-blade. I never go anywhere without my knife. A pair of black jeans. They belong to Wendy. Skin tight she wears them. I just start cutting. It feels good. What can I say? I do the same with her panties. Her shirt. The green loose-fitting shirt she wears with the sleeves rolled up, open at the navel. And as I go on to the others, I feel angrier and angrier. I try to imagine who they are. Rose, the one who wears the stupid heels. Tara, the brain. My teeth set on edge, my nose snarls back like some demented tiger. And then what's worse, I begin to realize I'm coming; it's bursting out of me like in a dream when you want to hold it back and you know it's just too late and it goes all over everything. And it feels just as good as a dream because that's the only way it ever feels good anymore. I kept feeling someone is going to walk in on me. I sneak out of the change room and leave school through an exit door on to the football field. I remember how bright the sun seemed to me; it hurt my eyes.

That was a dream. You see, there's nothing to understand about me and there's no use in trying; I'm a waste of time. Don't try to help me, man. Don't try to understand me. I'm like all those kids on the street, all the little boy and girl hookers and dope dealers and druggies. All of the bad ones. You can't help us any more than you can help all the little nigger kids you see on TV with flies in their faces and stomachs like watermelons. I don't really want your help. I love the pain and the hate; at least I can be sure of it. Just help yourself. I mean that. You should love your wife, your lady, a lot; love your children. Stick with them no matter what they do.

✧

"Joe." It's Kevin, from downstairs.

"Yeah?"

"Can you come down? There's a bunch of kids here to see you."

"Who are they?"

"Dunno. Say they're from school."

"Mister . . . Doctor, I didn't get your name. Look is it okay if I . . . Thanks. It's been nice talking to you." I call down. "Tell 'em just a minute, Kevin."

They came to see me? Gotta comb my hair. Christ I look like shit. At least four new zits since yesterday. Why do they want to see me?

"Kevin!"
"Whaa?"
"Come on up for a second."
Kevin comes up around the bend in the stairway. "Whadya want?"
"Are they all guys? You think it's a gang?"
"Two girls. Three guys. They got Christmas presents with 'em."
"Kevin, you're really funny. You know that?"
"Don't believe me." He starts back down.
I grab him by the collar of his sweatshirt. "Christmas presents? Hey, don't bullshit me."
"It's not bullshit, asshole. They're from the school, two girls, three guys, and they got presents. Now take your hands off me."
The shrink has come out on to the landing. I decide to follow Kevin downstairs. As I turn the bend in the stairs, there she is, Wendy. She's with her friend, Selima. The guys are there but I don't even see their faces. They're all wearing monster-sized overcoats. Spies.
"Hi, Joe."
"Wendy. Meet Kevin?" Kevin just walks away into the living room. I can hear the TV going, its lights and the Christmas tree competing, flashing off the glass doors.
"We miss you at school."
"Sure."
"No, we do. Don't we?" She half turns to the other four. Nobody says anything. I have to give her credit. She's an amazing girl. "Are you coming back after the break?"
"I been thinking about getting a job. I can't handle school any more."
"But you're so smart, Joe."
"Yeah."
"You are! Isn't he smart?" She turns again. They still don't say anything.
"It's nice of you guys to come over. Want to come in and sit down?"
"Joe, we just thought we'd stop by and give you these to put under your tree."
I start to explode. "You . . . you . . . ." No, I don't blame you. I wouldn't spend any time here if I didn't have to. I take the gifts. Two of them. Wrapped. Even ribbons. Something about the striped paper

and those goddamned green ribbons . . . I'm crying. Stupid Christmas gifts and I'm fucking crying. And they can see it. She puts her arms around me, the gifts between us pressing on my belly. She kisses me.

"Goodbye, Joe."

They go out. I take the gifts into the living room and throw them under the tree.

"S'matter, Joe?" It's Kevin.

"Goodbye, Joe. Merry Christmas."

It's the shrink putting on his coat, sticking out his hand for me to shake. I just turn away. "See you in the new year."

It's not until I come around the bend in the stairs that I can draw breath. Then, like blowing lunch, the sobs break out of me, my whole body shaking. Into my room. Under my bed, bits and pieces of old prescriptions, pain killer for my infected hand, Bobby's Valium, Halcion from when I couldn't sleep. And here I thought I didn't need this shit any more. One of each. I'm rational. A tape. Pink Floyd. *Comfortably Numb.* I lay face down on the bed which is still warm from when I was telling my life story. It doesn't take long. I'm awake.

It starts by hurting. It's going to end up hurting. But in between, if you're lucky, there may be something small and nice you can remember and you may find a way to forget.

THREE SOLITUDES

FIVE NIGHTS A WEEK FOR many years now, Sonia's mother had been cleaning up after old people, telling stories to the sleepless ones with their incomprehending smiles, carrying the frail bodies from bedroom to bathroom in her arms. Sonia would rush Grace out the door in the evening, admonishing her mother not to be late for her shift at the nursing home. Surely, unless the girl were an accomplished actress, she was now used to the necessity of her mother's absences. Then why, yesterday, did she hang on to the hem of her mother's uniform like some needy infant? Why, when Sonia was now eleven, had the panic of a two-year-old set in again?

She had always been a little strange and quiet, but, taken altogether, the past month had caused Grace to worry. The school was also concerned. She would often be heard talking to herself at the back of a classroom and, as if she had told herself some salacious joke, would burst into lewd laughter. She also laughed like that during Mr. Williams' funeral. He was her uncle, and, unlike other people in their community, the sum total of their extended family in Canada. She laughed in such a way that the usually mild Deacon asked for her removal. Darrell told Grace not to worry, that children sometimes laugh when they are uncomfortable. Grace knew all about that kind of laughter, how they try to hold it in and it bursts out of them. "This is different," she told her husband, "the girl is behaving like someone bewitched." Darrell dismissed this suggestion as part of an old world superstitiousness, abruptly terminating the conversation and walking out of the room. He wanted to be seen as a man on the rise, modern, industrious, working in the stockroom of a computer company by day and studying computer applications by correspondence at night.

Grace, undeterred, followed him to his study. "You think I need to work all night with this new baby in my stomach? I'm just going to quit if you don't pay her some attention." Annoyed as he was at this intrusion upon his work, he knew she meant it. He promised Grace that she could quit the day he finished the course and got a more highly paid position. That being said, he made a show about sitting down with Sonia to do homework before Grace left the house. Yet, Grace wondered, if Darrell's attention was what her daughter wanted, why did she grab on to her uniform?

There was more to the woman's uneasiness. Darrell had not touched her, his wife, for weeks. Last Sunday morning she dropped Sonia at the church, telling the Deacon that she and Darrell would return together later. She had arranged it so that she and her husband could for once be alone together. Despite her obvious efforts, he avoided her, wincing when she tried to massage his neck and shoulders. The thought crossed her mind that he may have found another woman, but then she reassured herself that he had no free hours in the day or night for an escapade. Then Grace recalled that the same thing happened when she was visibly pregnant with Sonia. This memory provided her with a measure of comfort, if only that it was better to understand a situation than to keep wondering about it. Once again, however, she imagined the girl's panic-laden eyes staring up at her and the thin hand holding the hem of her uniform. What did it mean?

✧

The girl's behaving like a fool. She's lightheaded. She laughs like a damned fool at everything. What does she find so funny all the time? Her uncle's death? Is that supposed to be funny? Why did you ever think you could trust her? And that woman, what does that old hippo want from you? "Got any suggestions, Darrell?" Suggestions. She bothers you with suggestions. I'll suggest that Sonia see Dr. Whalley for a check-up. Get the hippo off my back. Maybe not a doctor. Deacon Holmes might be better. Hypocrite Holmes. "My daughter has been acting strangely, Deacon Hypocrite. You remember . . . at the funeral? Can you see if she's got the Holy Spirit in her? Maybe she's getting the gift from God, Deacon." He'll buy that.

God. It must be He wants it this way. He's playing with you. Laughing, yes, He's laughing at you. He's got you over a barrel. Shit. Wear your navy suit when you go to see the Deacon. You look good in that suit. A white shirt. Striped tie. Play the respectable family man. That's what everyone thinks anyway. God knows . . . but what difference does it make? He can't do a damned thing about it.

Everyone's up to something. Take that Deacon Hypocrite. He's got that choir singing so well. Any man who spends that much time with a choir has to be doing it for the women or the boys. You can see it in his eyes.

✧

The Chinese man on the television cooks with a wok. Cuts everything up small, heats the wok, pours in oil, throws the food around. Cooks fast. Sonia's mom cooks slow. Sonia can smell the curry on the stove. Mom's gone. To work. Leaves the curry to cook for her husband and Sonia. The apartment is overheated, but Sonia, on the couch in front of the television, wraps herself in a blanket to watch the Chinese man cook. She hears her father get up from his desk and start to walk around. He goes into the kitchen, removes the pot lid, tastes the curry. She hears him in the kitchen, singing: "Itty bitty pretty one . . . . " The Chinese man is making almond soup now. White and milky. Good for Chinese dessert. Her father comes out in his black silk robe with two elegant red roses crossed at the stems embroidered on the right front chest, comes out to sit with Sonia on the couch. She thinks this time will be different. She thinks he will be gentle and fatherly. She will forget the last time and the times before that when, weeping on his knees, he promised it would never happen again.

He puts his arm on Sonia's shoulder; she draws the blanket tightly around her. He takes the edge of the blanket, momentarily unwraps her, then encloses himself in the blanket as well. She thinks he may be trying to get close to her again, father to daughter. Those other times were some kind of madness, he had said. Under the blanket, together, he lifts her gently on to his lap. She thinks, "No, it wasn't a mistake." Gently again, he can be gentle, she feels his hand beneath her skirt, feels him slide her panties down around the ankles, brushing lightly by her feet and toes. Then his fingers are between her legs, touching her lightly, almost a tickle, and then suddenly, painfully darting inside. Like last time. Pulling her face around, his mouth comes down on to hers. A long kiss. She, in pain, can barely breathe, neither can she struggle. Like a recurring natural disaster, a tornado or an earthquake, it is futile to resist.

"Does it hurt?" The voice comes to her out of the whirlwind. She shakes her head from side to side. "It's your fault, you know. You're so damned beautiful, big almond-eyed girl. Tell me when it hurts." It is always the same. Two fingers now, it must be. Deeper and more painful. She cries out. "Hurt?" he asks. She nods. She has to admit it hurts her. "Hurt? Hurt? Hurt? Hurt?" Why does he keep asking? Then an enormous grunt. He pushes her away. "Shit!" he says, "What are you doing to me, girl? Going to tell your mother what you're doing to me." He walks away, not even looking back. There is no begging for forgiveness this time. "Clean yourself up," she hears. Blood. She thinks he has wounded her.

✧

Grace returned at her usual time, an hour after midnight. She looked in on Sonia who appeared to be sleeping placidly, placed her fingertips on her daughter's wide warm forehead, and stroked just above the eyebrows. Then she kissed her on the cheek. "My strange and beautiful girl," she thought. And suddenly Sonia's arms were wrapped around her neck.

"Mom," she heard, a muffled voice. "Stay with me a while."

This daughter of hers was getting so foolish, staying up 'til all hours. "What's the matter, Sonia?" Grace tried to break loose, but was surprised by the desperate strength of the girl. "You go to sleep! How're you going to get to school in the morning?" Exhausted from the demands of the nursing home and craving the comfort of a hot bath, she nonetheless laid down on her daughter's bed. Dozing off in the dark silence she was awakened by Sonia's hands pushing against her and the words, "Get away! Get away!" Sonia's open angry eyes visible in the half light negated her mother's first impression, that her daughter must be dreaming. No, this had gone on long enough. She would speak to Darrell in the morning and they would come to some decision about what to do.

✧

Bald old bugger, what's he thinking behind those wire-rim glasses and that smile? Any man who looks that pious has got something up for sure. He's looking at you strangely. "Talk to my daughter. See what's the matter with her. I'll wait out here and pray, Deacon." Now that was smart, Darrell. Extremely smart. The father sits in the church to pray, comes all the way in the first snowfall to pray for his daughter's soul. Someone is trying to bewitch her. Deacon Hypocrite knows all about bewitchers. He knows what the congregation talks about when they leave this church. The Deacon is going to take one look at this respectable father sitting in the pew in his fine navy suit, his hands clasped together. He's going to scold the fools: "Does anyone know who has bewitched this poor man's daughter? We beseech the Holy Spirit to intervene."

As long as you're sitting here you might as well pray, Darrell. Pray the Holy Spirit will help a man not to feel such and such a way about his daughter. God will know you tried.

✧

Sonia knows there was no mistake and that it will happen again. She is shameful, disgusting. Why should anyone help her? The Deacon told her not to be a source of worry for her parents. Then he continued in his soothing voice. "Have you had visions, my dear? Have you been frightened by things you have seen in your heart? They may be gifts from God, Sonia." She is wrapped in her blanket again in front of the television. The Chinese man is talking about tofu tonight. He chops it neatly into little blocks. Green and red peppers, garlic, onions, chopped meat. *Ma po tofu*.

Her ears are also in the kitchen where her father is tasting the curry. "Itty bitty pretty one . . . ." She wishes he would go back to his desk. He comes in. Over his shirt and slacks is the black silk robe with the two red roses. He touches her face. He smiles at her. She cannot smile back although she knows that is what he wants, just as she knows what is about to happen. He wants a smile from her heart to let him know that everything is all right. Again she recalls the Deacon's voice. "Have you seen things in your heart, my dear, and then had them happen later on? That too is a gift from God, Sonia. It is called prophesy." He opens his belt. He pulls off his pants. He takes down his shorts. "This gets you in the mood." She hears the Chinese man turn the tofu in the wok, a scraping sound, not unpleasant. He laughs when he cooks. He is a happy man.

"You need to get in the mood." He reaches beneath the blanket, takes her hand out and makes the hand touch his sex. It rises up to crow like a rooster. A cock. Now she knows why the children call it a cock. She laughs. "You think it's funny? You always think everything is funny." He unwraps the blanket and lays her on the couch, keeping the blanket beneath her. The cock rams against her but it cannot go in. "Come on, laugh. You think it's funny." His mouth sucks the nipples on her emerging breasts. His fingers probe, pry her, widen her. She groans in pain. "Is it funny?" She shakes her head. It is enough for him. The fingers and her pain are enough. She stares at the wallpaper, a black and white pattern called chicken wire. She feels something warm and wet on her stomach. Smells rubbery. "Look at what you did to me, Sonia." The Chinese man laughs and laughs.

◈

Sonia's condition seemed to have worsened since Darrell took her to Deacon Holmes. The pointless laughter had now become brooding silence. Grace decided, in the face of Darrell's violent opposition, to take some time off to see if her magic with the aged patients would have some effect on her daughter. On the first night, Sonia clung to her like an infant. Darrell simmered, talking under his breath. Then he ranted. "How're we going to pay the rent, woman, with you sitting around here like this? Don't forget, either, we've got another child on the way." Saying this seemed to give him another idea. "That's what this is all about. Sonia knows she's going to have to share this apartment with a new baby. The girl's jealous." Grace thought her husband might have hit upon the truth, but then she had given her daughter so little time of late that she sympathized with this need. "Darrell, go out. You need a night out."

◈

Where does the hippo think you're going to go? Do you have time for sitting in a bar with ignoramuses? Does she think you're going to a concert, to the ballet? The two of them are just going to sit there and hold each other. How long is this going to go on? Shit. Calm yourself, Darrell. You're starting to look like a jealous man. Try to get some work accomplished. You're falling behind now. You'll be a stock boy the rest of your life. Get your ass whipped. "Darrell, would you please find some of the old two-sided floppy disks?" 'Please,' they say. So damned polite when they whip your ass. Going to see whose ass is whipped when you get your bankroll together.

❖

Sonia likes the feel of the water. Very hot. She feels like sliding beneath the surface and going to sleep. It would be so easy. Tonight, her mom has gone to work. She says she cannot afford to stay home with Sonia every night. From the bathtub, she hears him walking. The floors creak in the apartment. "Itty bitty pretty one . . . . " The door opens. He pulls the bathtub curtain aside and stands there. Stares. "You need some help, Sonia?" She says nothing in reply, closes her eyes. He kneels by the side of the tub and soaps her up and down, a faintly pleasant sensation. Then—nothing—it's as if her body has suddenly emptied of feeling. "Is this death?" she thinks, hopefully.

He is still there, but she feels as though she has flown to the ceiling and, with the perspective of a housefly, is watching him soap this girl, Sonia, who is in the bathtub below. She is watching him rinse her body and help her step from the bathtub. She watches him dry her off carefully. She watches as he takes down his pants and shorts and lays the girl down on the bathroom floor. She sees the angry cock push into and finally bury itself inside the girl. She can hear a high-pitched sound like a telephone receiver left off the hook. She watches him thrust and finish, push himself up and turn away from the disgusting creature on the floor, turn away and leave it there. Her eyes rejoin her body as she vomits on to the floor and climbs back over the side of the bathtub into the still warm waters. She slides her head below the water and breathes in. Her body rebels, blasts, coughs, sneezes the water. She places her chin on the side of the bathtub. She cannot die.

❖

Grace returned to work. Much of her efforts at the nursing home now were useless, as she felt more like a patient in need of care than a caregiver. Her appetite was enormous, but she could not hold food down, and the less she had inside her the more the lassitude overwhelmed her bloated body. She wanted to be released, to spend the evenings quietly at home. She would happily do with less, borrow if necessary, but Darrell would torment her with his expectations, driven as he was by the memory of a proud father who had paid to send his son to an English boys' school.

She felt the stirrings of resentment. Darrell mumbled insults about her under his breath. Pretending not to hear him did not mean she was unaffected; the words struck her like the point of a spear. His eyes always gravitated to their daughter on the rare occasions, like a Sunday afternoon, when the three of them were in a room together. Needing him, Grace began to feel jealous of Sonia. She found herself screaming at her daughter for the smallest infraction, the state of her room, a spot on her dress. She would scream and then she would break down, hold Sonia in her arms, and beg her forgiveness. But the next day she would wake up exhausted, see her husband's eyes averted, and the cycle would resume: nitpicking, screaming, begging for forgiveness. She thought she would leave Darrell after the baby was born, but she quickly reconsidered. Darrell was better than most men she knew. He was still a responsible man and a loving father.

❖

She's your daughter. *Your daughter.* You know what that means. Beautiful innocent child and you are ruining her, Darrell. Off in a corner talking to herself. Shit. What the hell were you supposed to do? Used to show you all that love and affection. "Kiss me, Daddy, kiss me." Hand on your thigh. It's got to be for some purpose. And you didn't really hurt her last time. You tried to be considerate. What difference does it make, anyway? Might as well be you as some boy at school who'd get her pregnant and leave her on the street. Can't see that it makes a bit of difference. You're not the worst, far from it. People beat kids, kill them, tie them up in garbage bags. Lady across the street slaps her kids on the ears. Those kids can't hear too well. That's damage. What about the police? You're walking through the neighbourhood, minding your own affairs, and two of those white cars going about eighty slam to a stop, one in front, one behind you. They make you hold the wire fence, spread your legs out. Feel you up. A respectable man like yourself. "Man answering your description, sir," and so forth. Like hell. If you get a little power in this society, you can have some fun. That's all they were saying. Headmaster had a lot of fun. Made you take your pants down in front of everybody. Put you over a barrel. Tied your hands. Tied your ankles together. Hellfire coming up your ass. That's damage. Kids stand around watching. You tell me which is worse.

♦

He is serving spaghetti dinner in his black silk robe. "I thought you'd like it for a change, Sonia." He is being kind to her. Maybe it's finished now. He hasn't touched her tonight. His kindness brings tears to her eyes. If only he could always be this way, like a real father who loves and protects his children. He has a gentle man inside of him. He serves her grape juice while he drinks a small glass of rum. "How does it taste?" She likes it at first but there's an aftertaste and a warmth in her belly. He goes into the kitchen to cut up some salad. He sings to himself, "Itty bitty pretty one . . . ." Sonia's fork drops. She stares at the partly eaten plate of spaghetti. It's moving. Worms. She closes her eyes for ten seconds. Opens them again. Still the worms. She tries again, but the vision persists. He comes in and sees her staring. "What's the matter with you, girl?" She covers her eyes. "Are you sick or something?" He comes over and caresses her hair, puts a fatherly arm around her shoulder. "No!" she screams over and over. He grabs her sweater and yanks her up, knocking over the chair. "Stop this foolishness. Stop this damned crying! Stop it! Stop it!" She is lying on the floor; something must have hit her but she cannot feel it. "Shit, why did you make me do that?" He picks her up and helps her sit on the couch. "Don't be feeling sorry for yourself. You have a good life here." He forces her to look at him. He gets some ice from the freezer and wraps it in a tea towel. He applies the ice to her cheek. Her eyes are empty. "Why bother to treat you nicely?"

♦

Grace could not understand how the accident had occurred. Darrell thought Sonia must have walked into her bedroom door on the way to the bathroom. He said he was reading, heard a loud bang and ran in to find her passed out on the hallway floor. "She might have been sleepwalking," he further surmised. Sonia mutely assented. Grace, however, had been a nurse long enough to know about bruises. A wound such as this one would have necessitated a higher rate of speed than is usually attained by someone walking to the bathroom. Put together with all the other strange occurrences, Sonia was afraid that the girl had deliberately harmed herself in some way in order to attract attention. Moreover, there was little she could do now to help her daughter. Dr. Whalley, worried about Grace and the condition of the fetus, had told her to check into the hospital.

Darrell's reaction to her imminent hospitalization was unexpected and reassuring. He seemed buoyant. He told Grace not to worry, that the new baby was the important thing, and that he would take care to see that things ran smoothly in her absence. This change in Darrell, coming at a sensitive moment, renewed her love for him. They embraced for the first time in months. "Take care of Sonia," she pleaded. He gave assurances that he would do his best.

◇

What kind of foolishness is starting now? Coming home after a hard day's work and she's not here. Told her we would go to visit the hospital then eat some dinner out together. Shit. She played you for a sucker, Darrell. All smiles and nods, all the time thinking how she's going to run off after school and have herself a good time. Cat's away. You want to see your mother, girl, you better get home on time. No dinner out. You had your time on the town. You have to use strict discipline or lose control, Darrell. Headmaster knew that. Strict discipline. Has to be done so you love the pain, love the stick, love the arm that whips you. She's got to respond. You have to show her who's in control.

◇

Sonia has found a friend at school, Karen. They looked at each other and right away they both knew, not the who, the how, or the why, but the hurt. They are known by teachers as "the two girls with the coats," winter coats worn in classrooms like suits of armor. They sit across from each other in a dimly lighted pizzeria, sipping the water from the melted ice of long ago finished glasses of Coke. Both girls are late; both will face the wrath of home, but neither girl can bring herself to leave the other.

"Told the sucker he better not try it again. I'll have him busted even if he is my brother. No way I'm gonna take any more from him. They got this clinic at the General, see? Lady doctors? Gonna show 'em my bruises and whatever else I get off the sucker. They call the cops for you."

"But your family? . . . "

"Their tough luck, see? They're not helping me any, are they?" Karen bites her upper lip and covers her mouth with an involuntary gesture. Her feelings have not yet fully hardened.

Sonia reaches out her hand and touches the trembling fingers across from her. This act of offering sympathy gives her, for the first time, an awareness of inner strength. "You're brave, Karen."

Her friend smiles, revealing a battle scar: a chipped tooth. "Thanks. What are you gonna do, Sonia?"

"Oh, I'm not like you . . . brave, that is."

"You still need help."

"My mom's in the hospital. I'm supposed to go see her this evening." She gets up to leave, thinking of her lateness and her father's anger. Nonetheless, she hesitates.

Karen holds her hand and stares into her eyes. "We could go down to the clinic together and help each other, see?"

"I want to, but I can't. Not yet, anyway." She justifies her inaction by thinking that she is better off than her girlfriend.

Sonia leaves Karen at the door of the restaurant and runs off through the cold streets, slipping often on the ice patches left by careless homeowners. When she arrives, he is at the window behind a slowly moving curtain. She sees him from the front walk better than he can see her. The door opens. He is trembling. "Where have you been?" She says she was with a friend and forgot about the time, then asks him how soon they are leaving for the hospital. "You've lost your chance. There's got to be some discipline around here." There are no preliminaries.

He yanks at her ski parka, jams the zipper in his impatience, and finally pulls it over her head. He puts his hand beneath her skirt, squeezes her there, picks her up and lays her down on the couch. "Don't you disappear from me this time. You be right here, Sonia." Her face begins to empty, eyes glazing over. "Get back here, Sonia. You're not going away this time. I'll kill you if you try that again." Her face fills with fear and hate. "Good. Good. Just as long as you're here. You're going to get into the mood this time." She can feel the angry cock burn into her. Her only line of defense destroyed, she sinks into surrender. "That's it, baby." When he pulls out of her and turns away, she is aware of pain. "You never be late again, you understand?" he says to the wall, unable to face her. She wants to hold him to her for comfort, but she throws up on the floor instead. Then she remembers the Deacon's words again. "Accept the Holy Spirit in your heart, my dear, and your sins will be drowned in the sea of forgetfulness." She repeats the words to herself over and over.

❖

Grace's first impulse in the hospital was to feel guilty for abandoning all the people to whom she was responsible, her husband, her daughter, her patients. After a week, she stopped thinking every day that she had to leave tomorrow. The trace of a smile appeared on her face. She would stay until she had the baby. Darrell and Sonia seemed to be doing fine, although their visits were less regular than she would have liked. He promised, however, to be there for the duration of the delivery, and that, she thought, would be enough. Her room was semi-private, cut in half by a beige plastic curtain, behind which was another expectant mother (the second since Grace had arrived) having a problematic pregnancy. The anxious family who visited this woman was more than enough company for Grace, who had begun to enjoy the luxury of being cared for and alone.

❖

What has she done? Talking to school authorities. The Deacon probably put her up to it. Or maybe that friend of hers. The two of them imagining all kinds of things together. Sonia lies. She has always been a liar. But you, Darrell, are one clever man. You put the doubt into The Children's Aid, a little hole of doubt you'll be able to drive a truck through by the time you're finished. They thought you were one of those uneducated fools. "I'm sorry to hear she would say something like that, ma'am. I can't imagine where she got such an idea, but I can see why you must be concerned. We've been quite worried about her mental state. I suggest you speak to Deacon Owen Holmes, Evangelical New Testament Assembly." A tone of respect came into the conversation. Shit. Put her in custody . . . for the time being. Shit! "We have to, Sir; the law gives us no choice."

You have to deal with the woman when she gets back from the hospital. Tough blow all around. "I think she's lost her mind, Grace. You wouldn't believe the things she's saying. I . . . no, 'we abuse her,' she's saying." Allegations.

This is your nightmare, Darrell. You remember now . . . a creature in the doorway, face in darkness, bright fire behind, fringe of coarse black hair like a boar's all around the head, and that naked body, fierce and angry. A voice tells you: "Protect Sonia from . . . the wolf man." You . . . of course it's you.

They're going to check her body. They're going to see what's happened. You're going to get your punishment. Going to get your ass whipped. Nothing else is going to do. Going to break you, make you plead for mercy, make you kiss the hand that whips your ass. You are going to get on your knees and thank the hand that kills the beast.

◆

Sonia comes to church. She has heard about her baby sister and wants to see her.

Shall we gather by the river,
The beautiful, the beautiful, river . . .

She sits in a small space at the end of the third pew. Her mother is to Sonia's right in the second pew holding the baby. Her father is there next to her mother, one seat over. The baby is in a swaddling blanket; Sonia cannot see her face but she hears little gurgling noises. She wants to reach out, take the baby in her arms and kiss it. Grace, feeling her daughter's intense stare behind her, turns slightly. The eyes of mother and daughter meet. Mother turns away, bringing the baby down so that Sonia cannot even see the bundle anymore. A sigh escapes the girl as the choir sings of hope.

> *Soon we'll reach the shining river,*
> *Soon our pilgrimage will cease,*
> *Soon our happy hearts will quiver*
> *With the melody of peace . . .*

In her mind, she sees a place where all the unhappy people of the world are embracing in the spirit of love.

Members of the congregation are filing out of the pews. Her family goes past. There is no remorse in his eyes. His hand reaches out to prevent her from coming close to see the baby, then others come between. By the time Sonia steps outside, they are half a block away. She stands in the cold street in front of the window of the church, crying. As the crowd disperses, she is left alone. Deacon Holmes notices her, picks up her chin and addresses her smilingly. "My dear, Sonia, do not let them separate you from your family. You will be better off at home. You are only feeling the terrible sorrow of separation."

◆

Darrell drove Grace and the baby home from the hospital. Naturally, she asked for Sonia. He talked of how their daughter had become a stranger, how he had begged her to come to her senses if only for her mother's sake and, all else failing, how he had prayed for her recovery in the church. "Those things she said about me, Grace . . . it hurts so much to have a child say such things about her own father." Then he explained how the Children's Aid workers had removed her from the house. "These social workers want to break up families. They don't ask any questions; they just come in and remove our daughter," dropping the "our" in there at the strategic moment to see if Grace was his ally or his enemy. It was during a minute of silence between traffic lights that Grace allowed her thoughts to go beyond what he was saying. No . . . with the baby asleep on her shoulder, Grace just knew that Darrell was a loving father. Sonia had to be imagining the whole story.

"We'll get her back when they know the truth, Darrell."

❖

Sonia has come home. She has denied she was ever abused. She has told the workers that she was jealous of the new baby and wanted more attention for herself. She is very sad she caused so much suffering and confusion. She got the whole idea from her friend, Karen. Karen's brother did terrible things to her and they removed her. It was a stupid thing to do and she is sorry. Deacon Holmes convinced her to tell the truth. She loves her parents and her new sister. Her mother is shaking her head in bewilderment, but shedding tears of joy. Sonia cannot live without her baby sister and her mother's love.

❖

It's only a matter of time. She can't talk to you, Darrell, not yet. She won't even look your way. You wouldn't think she's sorry about what she did. She should be sorry. Worrying her mother like that. In a matter of time you'll be back inside, inside that tight little . . . ooooh. Shit! You are one sick man, Darrell. But why'd He make it feel that way, so good, if it's not supposed to happen? Why'd she come back to you, a lamb to the slaughter? The social worker was annoyed at her. She thinks the girl's a liar. Lady, she tells lots of lies. Nobody knows the truth from the devil anymore. It's all confusion. In a matter of time, Darrell, she'll be eating out of your hand, begging for it. Under your control. This time, no one's going to believe her.

❖

Sonia has been a model daughter, helping with her baby sister. Tonight, leaving Sonia with feeding instructions, Grace went back to work. Sonia rests on her bed; alongside is the baby's cradle. When the baby awakens, Sonia changes her diaper and gives her the bottle, singing, as if it were a lullaby, the soothing song she remembers from the church:

> *Shall we gather by the river*
> *The beautiful, the beautiful, river . . .*

She thinks the baby is smiling for the first time. She hums the song. The floors creak. He is walking through the apartment. She sings louder so as not to hear, but when she takes a breath his voice slips in upon her consciousness. "Itty bitty pretty one . . . . " Naked, he enters the room, takes the baby from her arms, and gently lays her back down into the cradle. Deprived of her older sister, she begins to wail violently. As Sonia bends down to comfort the baby, he pulls his older daughter into his arms and begins to kiss her lips devouringly. The baby's wails are all she hears as he pulls off her clothes, throws her on the bed, and lies atop her. And when the long pent up river flows into her, all she hears is uninterrupted wailing. The baby. The baby. The baby. Those cries fill her with fear for the helpless being in the cradle and with hate, pure, endless and unforgiving, for the man who has tried to destroy her.

"Take care of your sister," she hears him say in parting. As suddenly as he arrived, he is gone, back to his work desk.

Sonia takes up the baby in her arms, feeds and comforts her, then puts her down to sleep. "Little sister, will you understand that I am doing this for you?" Slowly, she puts her clothes back on. Quietly, she puts on her winter coat and her boots and slips out the door. Walking four short blocks, she arrives at the hospital, ready to be examined.

SUPERINTENDENT'S SON

FRIDAY NIGHT. ICE PELLETS struck like flying needles against the windshield. Russell, mesmerized by the high-pitched monotony of the wipers, found himself recalling last night's dream. Awaiting his cue behind a curtain, dressed in tights, doublet, and a cape, he had forgotten the role he was about to play. Panic. Turning east on to Lawrence Avenue, the Dodge skidded to a stop, barely avoiding a big overcoated man who was slowly negotiating his way through the slush. In the lamplight, his face was ghastly and snarling. He retaliated for the near miss by banging his fist down on the hood of the car. Driving on, shocked and chastened by this bizarre attacker, Russell gave momentary attention to the road.

Before he had left the house, his trick of avoiding problems had begun to desert him. In the past, he could beam aboard the *Enterprise* and disappear into the dark silent comforts of outer space. Now, he had begun to brood. He could blame Saunders for that. His parents' divorce had only yesterday become official. True, they had always had their spats, escalating dialogues that would never quite rise to the level of shouting. The Superintendent, as he called his father, used to point out flaws in his mother, some stupid thing like the yellow on her teeth. She was never secure enough to ignore his nitpicking. Sometimes they would argue about Russell, with each accusing the other of spoiling their only son. While there was no memory of a time when the family had ever lived happily together, the separation six months previous had caught Russell and his sister off guard. One day his father had said matter-of-factly,

"It seems I can't live with your mother any more." The next day he was packing his things.

"Why now?" Russell had asked, helping him load a box full of books into the trunk. "I mean I know Mom has always been a pain..."

"Your mother's a good person, Russell. I mean that, and I want you to help her as much as you can."

No, he knew his father didn't believe that. It was her fault... and also his own, the mess he was making of his life. The beginning of the end, though, was his mother's foolish insistence on comparing the Superintendent to her own father. Going on about Grandpa like that, "loving," "loyal," full of "the old-fashioned virtues," had been a mistake. And why say those things to the Superintendent, of all people?

Russell's twin sister, Jesse, the prodigy, the musical genius who studied the violin at university, sided with her mother. She recounted to him in detail how Mother had tried to change herself to suit her father's tastes. He had wanted her to be elegant. Then he wanted her exotic. Then Western. Italian skirts, Indonesian earrings, cowgirl hats. Nothing could ever please him for very long.

"Sure he's critical," Russell had told his sister on the telephone. "He's critical of everyone, except you, maybe. Remember how he used to get on me for spilling my juice or jumping the lines of my colouring book? I learned to live with it."

"He's in no position to be critical."

"Don't tell me that you're gonna start getting down on Dad."

Jesse changed the subject, saying how depressed she was without anyone around to talk to. He had a feeling that his sister was holding something back, but he felt sorrier for himself, stuck at home with his mother.

"I don't see why I can't live with Dad."

"Mother needs you right now, Russell," she said with tears in her voice.

God, how he hated female sentimentality! "That's easy for you to say. You're away at school."

"It's your own fault you're still at home."

Well, she was right about that. Maybe if he made an effort at school, his father might be persuaded to have him on a permanent basis instead of visits on alternating weekends. Since he'd moved out, Russell's father had loosened up. He'd bought him this car and let him have his own key to the new apartment. If only the Superintendent could learn to be a little less restrictive around television watching.

He was stopped at a traffic light. "Beam me up, Scotty." Late, as usual. Why hadn't he started out earlier? Marni would be angry. Despite what she thought, it was not his intention to make her angry. He liked her, her deep voice, her sincerity, the perfect little gifts she gave him, like the Adonis-shaped bottle of cologne that must have taken her an hour to wrap. Tonight she was making dinner for him and her parents. He could see in his mind the congealed food and the unconcealed disappointment in three faces. He could hear the tirade begin.

Why couldn't she just get off his case? He had given up going to his father's until tomorrow and was driving through sleet in order to see her family. That had made sense to his mother, who was happy to see her son taking an interest in this girl. The problem was, he really wanted to go over to Noah's where he could watch Star Trek reruns on his friend's enormous video screen. Marni hated Star Trek. If it weren't for the Superintendent and his ideas about television not being 'quality time,' he would probably have gone to his father's, notwithstanding the fourteen-inch television set. "This is what comes," he thought, "of trying to please everyone but myself."

"Uhuru! Chekhov! I'm lost down here in Scarberia! Beam me up, for chrissake!" Instead of rescue, another Gorgon's head pushed itself into his consciousness. Miss Halliday had given him an extension to hand in an English essay. One more week. Probably because his father told her that Russell was in treatment. The extension now felt like a major disappointment. *For Whom the Bell Tolls* was sitting on his desk, unopened for the whole week. This was Canada, after all, and they had to read American novels. He was thinking of refusing to do the essay as a protest.

Not that he was averse to spending time in the school library. Certain things appealed to him, like the smell of the books and the personality of the librarian, Mr. Farnham, who sometimes joked with

Russell about *Star Trek*. "Warp Two, Scotty!" he would call out from behind the circulation desk.

"Aye, Captain, I'm givin' 'er all she's got."

Russell noticed that the librarian would never miss an opportunity to joke with him. He found this type of repartee a refreshing change from the moralizings of overly serious adults. If he fell asleep at his study carrel, he might be awakened by a tap on the shoulder. "Careful now, Russell, you wouldn't want to strain your eyes."

"That's precisely why I'm resting, sir."

Remembering this exchange gave Russell his first decent idea of the night: he would start wearing dark glasses to school. When questioned about it he would say that he had an eye muscle problem just like his father. What was it called again? A stigmatism? He could get considerable mileage from such an excuse. If he ever did manage to finish the paper, Halliday might give him high marks for his effort.

This new ruse recalled to him the way he began the semester with a heavily bandaged foot and a pair of crutches borrowed from Noah. He laughed aloud remembering his late arrivals and the concerned faces of the office staff who readily excused him. It would have worked for the whole semester if the vice-principal hadn't seen him chasing Marni Sims across the parking lot of the local shopping mall on the Saturday afternoon before Thanksgiving. Ms. Deal made a point of stopping her car, rolling down the window, and commenting about his speedy recovery. "Ma'am," he remembered saying, "the doctor told me to keep my weight off it until he could examine the x-ray. He called on Friday and told me I had nothing to worry about." He was sure by the way she smiled that the vice-principal admired his coolness under pressure, the skill and timing of his delivery. But she said, "We'll see, Russell."

He knew she would call his mother to verify the story of the crutches. His mother of course knew nothing about the crutches or the doctor. Ms. Deal, rubbing her hands together, called Russell into her office on Tuesday and confronted him with the evidence of the charade. From the start, he stared insolently at a bra strap which poked out from the wide neck of her dress. A quick look down and she knew, all right, but she could not bring herself to adjust it in his presence. It provided just enough of a distraction. "I know you called her, Ma'am.

You upset her. The truth is I didn't want her to know about the possibility that I had fractured my foot. I took the bandage off every day before I came in so that she wouldn't worry. You had absolutely no reason to call her, and no right, if I may say so." Ms. Deal, her face going red, then asked for the doctor's name. "He's at Toronto General, orthopedics or something. I think his name was Berg or Gerber. I'm not really sure." Russell remembered smiling broadly, while continuing to stare directly at the strap.

As he got up to leave the office, she had stopped him with her loud voice. "Truth. Does that matter to you at all, Russell? All these stories and fabrications begin to add up. One day you won't know the difference between truth and lies. Don't you see what that means?"

"You mean like *The Twilight Zone*?"

Breathing out heavily, she said, "I want a letter from that doctor."

"I guess I'll go over there and look for him." And then to himself he had added, "And I'm sure not to find him."

"It's time you did something with your life, young man." She banged her fist on the desk for effect. "Your father can only do so much for you . . ."

Before he could escape, it turned into another pull-up-your-socks-this-is-for-your-own-good lecture. How pathetic she was! Same for all of them. Like his mother with her old-fashioned virtues. The dark glasses, he thought, would add another chapter to his illustrious educational career. And the fools would know better than to question him this time.

This trip to Marni's was taking forever. Really, sitting down to dinner with the Simses just wasn't worth the effort. Noah lived over there behind the shopping mall on Markham Road. The wheel of the car just happened to turn in the direction of his friend. At last. "What took you so long, Scotty? Klingons zap the power source?"

✧

"Are you listening to me, Russell? Did you hear what I just said?" Mrs. Warren emphasized each word as if making little Morse code dots with a pen pointed at her son's face. Her son had come back from his date unexpectedly early and she was not going to let this opportunity get away.

"My last chance, right?" Russell asked, pushing the annoying pen to one side. He wished his mother would start acting like a wimp again.

"Sometimes your eyes get that faraway look."

"Don't worry. I'm getting my act together this time, Mom."

"I'll believe that when I see it. Nineteen years old and you're still behaving like a child. Why don't you listen to Dr. Saunders?"

Russell put both thumbs under his armpits, moving his elbows up and down. "Quack, quack, quack, quack, quack."

Mrs. Warren saw in Russell's mockery her husband's attempts to undermine the therapy sessions. "I know he's tough on you, but he has your best interests at heart."

"Yes, he's doing it for me and he hates making money."

"Tell that father of yours that some things are worth the price."

"You're always getting on Dad, running him down every chance you get."

"You're right, Russell. I promised you I wouldn't. I can't tell you how hard it is to keep my word." Then she added, "I don't care what you think of me . . . or Saunders; it's positively your last chance. No one, not even your father, is going to rescue you. I hope you're listening, Russell."

Russell did not have to listen this time. Dr. Saunders had recommended putting all agreements in writing, having them signed, and hanging them in prominent places. A list of Russell's responsibilities and a weekly calendar had been magnetized to the refrigerator:

1. I will search for a part-time job.
2. I will attend all my classes at school.
3. I will do my homework.
4. I will do my household chores.
5. I will attend my therapy sessions.

Below the list appeared an ultimatum.

> Failure to follow through on any of my responsibilities or continued failure at school will result in my leaving home.

"Sign it here," his mother said, holding out the ball point pen and pointing to an underline marked by an *x*. Russell had a very distinguished looking signature, having had practice at school in the signing of agreements. He took the pen from her and with a flourish signed his name. The signing itself made him feel as if he had already followed through on the responsibilities.

The refrigerator was chosen as being second only to the television screen as a place for Russell to focus his eyes. She might also have chosen to tape the agreement to the bathroom mirror had she known about the hours her son spent anxiously searching his complexion for telltale signs of age. Nineteen years old and he had not even begun to shave. When Russell went out with Noah, the smooth-faced appearance of the two belied their four-year difference in age.

Was it this youthful look and his cute touch of plumpness that allowed him to continue on in high school when other students his age had already been shown the door? Almost every teacher in the school had failed him once. He had obtained a handful of credits from those who had him a second and a third time and who tired of chasing him, calling his father and mother, or listening to his never ending stream of excuses for absences, failures, and incomplete assignments. Not that it hurt being the Superintendent's son.

After his father had moved out, his mother slowly began to change. Much as the Superintendent liked to think of himself as the brains in the family, Mrs. Warren had also been a successsful student at the University of Toronto. Hadn't she 'helped' her future husband with several essays? Hadn't she tutored Jesse? These memories gave her the confidence to look for solutions to her son's problems, insisting that Russell see the family doctor. After ruling out double vision, hearing loss, dyslexia, bouts of nervousness or depression, and insomnia (surely not), the doctor recommended that Russell see Dr. Saunders, a noted adolescent therapist.

Dr. Saunders was locked in a chess game with Russell, trying to stay one step ahead of the cagey boy. He kept in contact with both parents, encouraging them to be more frank with their son. Now, from their respective distances, both began to state aloud what they, in their desire to blame the other, had never dared to say, things like "Russell is lazy," "selfish," "immature," and so forth. Moreover, the list of responsibilities and the ultimatum had now been posted on the refrigerators of both family home and father's apartment. Russell would be forced to see the agreement when he came into either kitchen to fix a snack. "Far better than nagging him," Dr. Saunders had said.

As Russell opened the refrigerator door, the telephone rang. His mother answered it. "Yes, right here in front of me, Marni, looking for something to eat." Mrs. Warren stared at her son's eyes peeking up over the refrigerator door. She shook her head and held out the receiver, whispering, "You didn't even see them?"

"Hi." Russell stared at his mother and waved at her backhanded, like a broom attempting to sweep her out of the room. He could hear crying from the other end of the telephone. Russell tried his best to parry. "Sorry. No, I really am. You don't understand. I know you did. I know, but Noah offered to help me with that English essay."

As always, Marni was tempted to believe he was telling the truth, but his failure to call her tipped the balance. "I'm not going to let you do that to me anymore, Russell."

"You mean you don't want to see me?" he asked, and in such a way that he sounded genuinely concerned. "Well, if that's the way you feel . . . . " Was that a feeling of relief going through his body? He went up to his bedroom and, adjusting himself into a comfortable position on his bed, flipped on the remote control for the television. He turned off the sound and listened to his two telephone messages. The first was from his father asking where he was. "Why don't you call if you're not going to make it? Forgive me, Russell, for expecting common courtesy." The second was from Marni, saying "never mind," she would leave the message with his mother.

All of them, they were all on his case. Damn that Saunders! That list was really starting to bug him. The part-time job was supposed to be a way for Russell to help out in the payments for his car. He decided to stop in at the mall every day after school to ask one or another store operator if any openings had come up. His friends had told him that times were tough, so he was sure the shopkeepers would just keep saying "no." Could anyone blame him for the state of the economy? Then he could drive home each day and check off the number one responsibility on his list while still being able to catch the late afternoon soap operas.

He had already shown progress in having attended a full week of classes. However, two of his teachers had said to him after the bell rang: "You are present in body only, Russell." Strange how both of them had said the same thing. They must be talking about him to each other in that staff room of theirs. Who really cared what they thought, anyway?

As to homework, well, the agreement did not state that he had to do all of his homework. Russell would do some homework, at least the parts that weren't boring. And household chores he would do now, saving them of course for a time when his mother was around and could actually see him working. These small signs together would give encouragement to his mother and allow his father to think that the money he was paying the therapist was well spent. Whenever his father felt that way, he would open his pockets to Russell for something more.

The very same agreement hung like a millstone on the bulletin board in Saunders' office. Did the guy leave it hanging there for others to see? Hatred, pure and simple, was what he felt for the therapist. The guy had some pet theory that Russell was afraid of standing on his own two feet. A complete know-it-all.

"Russell, you don't have an eighty in science. You couldn't add two subjects together and get an eighty. It's bullshit, Russell. Bullshit. You're up to your eyeballs in it," Saunders had taunted, revealing his copy of Russell's interim report card. No doubt the Superintendent had sent it to the therapist.

"Who is he, anyway?" Russell thought. "Nothing but an overgrown hippie who swears like crazy."

"Russell, let's get down to brass tacks. What were you supposed to do this week? The English essay, Russell, right?"

"I'll probably get around to that soon."

"Probably means never, Russell. Probably means never. Like maybe. You're going to fuck up again, aren't you, Russell? You want to fail, don't you? Well, I'm not going to let you fail, Russell." What bothered him even more than the swearing and the taunts was the numbing repetition of his name. Russell thought it might be some technique to hypnotize him. "Interesting, Captain. Perhaps you wish me to try a Vulcan mind read?"

✧

Saturday. His father's apartment had cavernous closets and built-in bookshelves, both of which spaces remained peculiarly empty. The Superintendent still lived out of the boxes and suitcases Russell had helped him pack six months ago. Every so often he would pick up his dirty clothing from the floor, wrap them in a used sheet, and drop the mess off at the dry-cleaner's on his way to work.

In counselling sessions, Dr. Saunders pointed out that it would be difficult to make Russell accountable for his actions if his father's personal life remained in a state of chaos. The Superintendent gave some vague assurances to the doctor, but he told his son the next weekend that "Saunders sticks his nose into everything."

Ringing the doorbell twice and getting no response, Russell had already taken out his keys before his father opened the door. That delay and the condition of the apartment gave Russell the idea he had not been expected. The chaos was definitely worse than usual. Some of the boxes in the living room had been overturned, their contents spilling on to the floor. A curtain sagged from its rod.

"How are things at the school?" he asked his son in an absent way. Russell noticed that the sloppiness had now spread to the Superintendent's clothing, old jeans he had worn last year while painting the garage, high-top sneakers, a white sweat shirt worn back-to-front with a red stain on the sleeve. His hair, recently tinted black, bent over like wheat in a windstorm. His eyeglasses were balanced precariously; his index finger kept having to prevent them from falling off his nose.

"Fine, as if you don't know." Russell's eyes kept returning to the stain. Was it blood?

"Staying out of trouble?" His father still made no effort to invite him inside.

Russell shrugged. Mr. Warren looked over his shoulder at the apartment and made a disparaging gesture. "Can you believe the mess in here?"

"What's happened, Dad?"

"When I didn't find you here after work yesterday, I assumed you decided to skip this weekend. The least you could have done is call me back. Tell you what," he said, reaching into his pocket and pulling out a crumpled ten dollar bill, "could you go down to Sue's and get me some Comet and a couple of sponges? What do you say to cleaning up this dump?" As Russell stood staring at him, he added, "Dr. Saunders wants me to get my act together . . . and you're supposed to help." Still Russell made no move to leave. "Hey, keep the change." He began to close the door in his son's face.

Staring hard at his father, Russell blocked the door with his foot. He was, however, unable to stare through him, so he took the money. "Okay, Dad, I'll be right back." His father's door closed as Russell walked over to the elevator and pressed the down arrow. When the bell rang and the door slid open, instead of getting in he ducked into the small room adjacent to the elevator where the garbage chute was located.

The stench was almost unbearable. Three small plastic bags full of garbage were at his feet. Fish. He stuffed the three bags one by one down the chute and, while it gave him a bit more space, it did nothing to relieve the smell. But he understood that his father would probably look out the door before sending anyone outside. That was it, all right. That's why his mother had blabbered on about the old-fashioned virtues. The Superintendent was getting laid. Hot and heavy, too, it looked like. Didn't know he had it in him.

Because the door to the room was made of steel, Russell could hear nothing except the elevator alongside going up and down the shaft. Suddenly, the door opened and another small white plastic bag of garbage flew in, hitting Russell just below the chin. "Hey!" he called out.

"Sorry," said a tall angular young man, his deep voice sounding more bothered than sorry. He had a wiry electric shock of blond hair that surrounded his rough round face like the rays of the sun.

Russell said, "I gotta stand here putting other people's garbage down the chute?"

"Fuck," said the other, shrugging his shoulders.

Feeling ridiculous, Russell emerged from the room, leaving the garbage bag on the floor. The young man pressed the elevator button.

Russell waited with him for the elevator, having decided to run his father's useless errand. On the long trip down, he stared at the young man, noticing beneath an open overcoat the wide collar of a silk shirt; on his feet were a pair of shiny expensive shoes. On the way back up from the shoes, Russell saw his long fingers pull up the zipper on the fly of his pants. He quickly looked up to the face again, where there was a hint of a smile. A small cut, like a shaving nick, became visible beneath the lower lip. Out in the cold air, the two walked away in opposite directions.

By the time Russell got to the corner store, he had forgotten the reason for his errand. He then took up a spot in front of the magazine stand and became absorbed in the latest issue of the *National Enquirer*. A small picture of Leonard Nimoy above the headline had attracted his interest. Inside the front page was a photo of a terribly gaunt man and an accompanying story, another former celebrity dying of AIDS. A rotating bubble of light from a passing police car flashed across the store. Halfway through the story, Russell stopped reading and placed the tabloid back on the stand. An observer would not have noticed a change in Russell's demeanour, but his stomach had dropped as if he were back on the elevator and it had gone into free fall. Maintaining an outward calm, he began to leave, but then felt the ten dollar bill in his pocket. Numbly, he bought some cleanser and a box of Jay Cloths.

Emerging from the elevator, he went back into the room with the garbage chute. The plastic bag was still on the floor. He undid the tie and opened the bag, gingerly fingering through the contents. Two crumpled Master Card receipts, both with his father's signature, confirmed what he already knew. He threw the bag down the chute and left the cleaning items and the change at his father's door.

Down in the apartment garage, he sat for a long time immobilized at the wheel of his car, the key in the ignition. His mind kept returning to the stink of that little room and to that plastic bag that had practically hit him in the face. "Beam me up! Beam me up! Don't leave me here, Scotty!"

A guttural noise began to come from him, gradually deepening to some part of his anatomy he never knew existed, emerging finally into a lion's roar. He sucked air into what had become the vacuum inside his body. When had he last taken a real breath?

Hands shaking, he pulled the keys from the ignition, got out, locked the car door, and rode the elevator back upstairs. His father had not yet taken the cleaning items in, so he dropped the keys inside the bag on top of the Comet. As he returned to the elevator, his father's door opened and his head popped out. He looked at his son. Then he picked up the bag and looked inside. Russell tried to keep his eyes on the elevator door.

"What's going on? Where're you going, Russell? The keys are here."

The elevator bell rang. The door opened.

"The keys!"

Russell got on, pressed G, and the door slid closed.

Hatless, bootless, in a light jacket, the cold wind of the street burned his face and ears. He passed a few pedestrians walking the long three blocks from the subway. One was an old man with a cane whose body was bent sideways in the wind. He was not wearing a hat either. Russell was amazed that this man, battling on like some maimed insect, was able to move ahead and not be blown down to the sidewalk. A brown girl, rivers of tears down either side of her face, ran past, glancing behind her. Who was she running from? "Need help?" he heard himself say. She sped on, oblivious to him. Across the street, a bag lady was trying to push a shopping cart. She seemed lost, like a polar bear on an ice floe.

He called Marni from the telephone at the subway. Her mother answered, and after saying his name so that her daughter would know who was on the line, told Russell she had gone out. "Look, I know she's there. I have to talk to her." Marni's mother politely told Russell that her daughter would "probably" call him back later. "Damn that Saunders!" he said to himself, hanging up, remembering the therapist's words, "Probably means never, Russell." Oh, how he had toyed with people. How small the stakes seemed now.

He went home. His mother was on the telephone. She looked at Russell for a moment then went on talking. For the first time, Russell realized that her social life had gone into neutral since the separation. She used to entertain the Superintendent's school board acquaintances. What did she do now for fun except talk to Jesse and her father on the telephone?

Russell went up to his room and turned on the television. Nothing was on except sports, so he put on a *Star Trek* video. The magic was gone. An episode he had seen fifty times, where the Klingons take over the *Enterprise*, suddenly seemed flat and predictable. The stilted dialogue, the ridiculous sideburns, the polyester outfits, the whole thing was laughable. And this is what he had lived for, had talked about endlessly with Noah as if it made the two of them privy to the secrets of the universe. He turned it off and waited until he heard his mother hang up the phone.

They met each other on the stairs.

"Why'd you leave the car, Russell?"

"That was him?"

His mother nodded.

"I'm not taking anything from him any more."

"Should we give up the house, too? And what about your clothes? You're being foolish."

"But he lied to you . . . and to me."

"No, he didn't lie. He just never told you. I told him not to say anything."

Russell took a moment to absorb this revelation. He felt he had the right to be angry. They had treated him like an infant and he had blindly gone along. Willingly, as well.

"What good would it have done?"

"Shut up! I don't want to hear any more!"

"What difference does it make, anyway? Russell, he's still your father. Stop crying and go get your car."

He was disgusted with her for making light of the whole thing. Giving up that car was the first morally pure thing he had ever done in his life. Or so he had thought. He was not about to cheapen that gesture by an immediate about-face. "No, Mom, it's time for me to get some work done."

"Really?" she laughed.

"There's nothing funny about this," he said, and then, despite himself, remembering the ridiculous moment at the garbage chute, he burst out laughing. "Goddammit!" he shouted, stopping the laughter abruptly.

Smiling, she put a hand on his shoulder. "Why don't you go talk to him? He loves you and I think you love him."

"Really, Mom, I need some help with that English essay."

"Have you read the book?"

"Kind of."

"Read the book first."

Read the book. How boring. His righteous feeling gone, he turned and went back up the stairs. Hemingway, old grizzle beard, was waiting there for him on his desk. It was only Saturday afternoon. Maybe he would read the first chapter. It would be a start.

HORROR FILM

A CROWD FROM THE SCHOOL came to the cemetery for Ali's funeral today. I heard some angry talk, but by now, this being our third student death of the year, they have learned how to behave themselves. Alana's father wisely kept her at home; it's safe to say we won't be seeing her again at the school.

The whole series of events, the coincidences, the random violence, and the inevitable conclusion, began right here in my classroom. They come at me like scenes from a movie in which my students are the stars and I, their teacher, am a supporting actor. But, like the boy in *A Clockwork Orange*, I am imprisoned, belted to the seat, my eyes propped open.

Close-up: the toe of a loosely tied red-sneakered foot resting on a brick. Fade to the young mixed-race couple, conservatively dressed, walking together past a large government housing project, the arm of the black man protectively around the shoulders of the white woman. Cross fade to the toe, tensing, pushing the brick forward. Eerie, ominous, music then sudden silence. Still close up: the ill-fated couple in their last happy moment together.

Alana Laing and Ali Rose were a throwback to my type of student—inquisitive, alive, prepared. Even their dress was anachronistic, she in tortoise-shell glasses, dark woollen skirt and white blouse, and he in gold wire-rimmed oval glasses, white shirt and silk tie. They ranted like parliamentary opposition members, she with her anti-welfare stance, her diatribes against big government, and he with his evolving ideas against global white supremacy. It sounded extreme, even simplistic at times, but at least their arguments had substance and passion! The others, the know-nothings, were too intimidated to do anything but stare resentfully. "The hell with them," I thought. What better way to bring home to them the ignorance of their television-stunted brains?

I saw a good deal of Alana's father. He was a shoe salesman who had seen his own business destroyed by free trade and had begun to live through his daughter's accomplishments. Somehow, he had managed to maintain his belief in hard work and the beauty of the marketplace. He came to me, as he did to all her teachers, to make sure Alana had extra homework. He was obsessed by tabloid accounts of teenagers mangled in car accidents, knifed at parties, swarmed by gangs, drug-addicted, raped, pregnant, and diseased, so he made sure she had no spare time. The mother had died of cancer when Alana was eleven, so, by seventeen, she had internalized her father's precepts and fears. He dropped her off at school at eight and picked her up at five-thirty. She spent most of her extra hours in the library, but every so often she would drop in on me to try out her latest right-wing views, hoping to convert me to her father's way of thinking. Even though I remained steadfast in my left-leaning liberal views, she would have sharpened another knife to throw at Ali, her only real rival.

Ali's real name was Alex Rose. Mr. Kurelovic, our gym teacher with tree trunks for thighs and a pea for a brain, imagined that the tall young man looked like Muhammad Ali. While he foresaw a basketball star, Ali would not allow himself to be typed, especially at our school where sports tend to be segregated. The fact that whites play hockey, Chinese play volleyball, and blacks basketball repulsed him. The nickname Ali was an ironic joke to his fellow students, but, knowing that his namesake was far more than a boxer, the young man accepted it with gratitude.

Ali confided in me because I accepted him for what he was and who he wanted to be. His parents, unassuming people, had wanted him to be a lawyer. I think they had envisioned something cool and secure for their son, but he started to smoulder when confronted by the daily slights and outright bigotry of Scarborough. He told me how his family went back one hundred and sixty years in Canada, yet well-meaning teachers asked him about hot curries, the islands, or made references to "your people." Adults he respected complained of rough treatment by the legal system and midnight visits from immigration officers. He had a few friends and he read the newspapers so he no doubt knew about the way police treated black people. One incident, however, bothered him more than anything he had heard second hand. It happened while his dad and he were driving to a ball game. As they waited at a red light, some yahoo screamed "nigger lips" at them. He told me about it in a state of controlled fury.

"I wanted to talk to my dad, but he pretended not to have heard. It hurt him as bad as it hurt me, but he just drove on and talked about how the Blue Jays needed a power hitter. In my mind was my mother's face, the every-day sadness and the hard-won dignity. I told him to drop me at the next corner. He pleaded with me to come to the game. 'Relax,' he told me, 'you have to learn to ignore that trash.' I'm not gonna relax."

That was quite a seminar, at least for the time the two of them were in there, Alana referring to Ali as "our wide-eyed radical" and Ali firing back at "the tool of racist oppression." I remember the day their strong words for the first time rang hollow. They looked into each other's eyes and saw what the other students had been seeing all along, that in reality they were mirror images, intellectual oddballs. I watched as the bridge of need crossed the gap of belief. Neither had been aware until then that the bitterness in their views had been fuelled by their isolation from those other young people. The growth of good feeling between them became translated into a less resentful view of the world. It seemed that Ali was either less bothered by racism or noticed it less.

Now, Alana and Ali could have the friend I think both secretly desired all along. They only needed a way to overcome shyness and hesitancy. Under the pretext of needing their help to prepare a major unit on Japanese militarism, I asked them to join me for a coffee at the mall behind the school. It just so happens that this coffee shop is where most relationships at our school are officially begun. Alana and Ali were aware of this fact, just as they knew about The Fox theatre and about 'the woods,' but my presence would provide them with a safety factor. Nonetheless, both came prepared to discuss Hirohito and God only knows what, so I took the liberty of excusing myself after fifteen minutes.

Alana wasn't ready for even the small amount of social life which ensued. Dominated as she had been by her father, she had also been forced to partake of his isolation. At times, I would see the young couple walking together in the mall, she unstudied and spontaneous, blushing, smiling at me broadly, maintaining a physical closeness to her boyfriend which observers might have felt inappropriate in such casual circumstances.

Ominous music resuming. The sneakered toe tensing. The couple walking past the housing project adjacent to the mall. Close-up: the toe pushing the brick beneath a balcony railing. Slow-mo shot of the couple and the falling brick: Ali seeing the brick and pulling Alana to the pavement. Blackout.

Jason Carr, the one who did it, was one little bastard. It was coincidental that I was the teacher who had had him suspended from school. To tell you the truth, I wanted no part of him from the beginning. How was I to teach history to some illiterate street kid? You get all types in your classroom in the public system, especially in the lower grades. They drop them at your door without a word of warning, and they expect you to teach them something. The situation forces you to prioritize. I wasn't about to sacrifice the other twenty-seven kids in that class. He went at me with interruptions from the opening bell, like a busy prize-fighter, asking question after stupid question. Then he went to the Principal and accused me of failing him on a test because of racism. Me. I mean I could understand if he had accused half the teachers on the staff, but not me. I was not about to let him get away with that. A lot of teachers shook my hand when they heard that Jason had been tossed out for throwing a punch at me.

I was in the hospital room when my brilliant, promising, happy Alana awoke forty-eight hours later, and, aside from a surface wound, appeared just the same as before. She recognized her father, Ali, and me sitting together uneasily. But something was very wrong. Why did she insist she had eaten lunch before it had been served? Why, when told she must be mistaken, did she break into tears? It was apparent to everyone but her father, with his capacity for self-delusion, that some mechanical function in her mind had been impaired or, as we now know, destroyed.

The three of us spent many evenings together in the hospital, although Alana's father always pointedly ignored Ali. Mr. Laing was impatient with his daughter, believing that a strong will was sufficient to overcome any problem. He had brought her schoolwork to make sure she would not fall behind. When she stared with bewilderment at the calculus as if it were Chinese characters, he pressed her to "make an effort." When her attempts failed and she broke into tears, he carried on like a drill sergeant: "Take hold of yourself, Alana!" He even looked at me for a second, perhaps thinking I might have some magical technique for unravelling the confusion. Then he threw up his arms, ran his fingers through his thinning hair, and turned to look out the window while Ali sat on the bed and held Alana.

Upon her release from the hospital, Mr. Laing redoubled his efforts to turn his daughter into a medical miracle. It seemed his life could have no meaning unless she became a prodigy again. The doctor had said something about her brain needing "new synapses," so he insisted that in the hours before and after school a Special Education teacher take her through all the curriculum she had lost. Both the teacher and Alana quickly discovered that relearning was easier in theory than in fact. Dates were especially confusing, as when she insisted that the Spanish Armada had been defeated in the Nineteenth Century. Debating points would slip away from her in mid-sentence. Eventually, she left my history seminar, but we maintained our contact outside of class. She came to me one day looking perplexed and exhausted.

"Mr. Pender, you've always been so helpful. I wanted to ask your opinion about something."

"Go ahead, Alana."

"It's about Ali. He wants to be . . . "—and here she fought for a word—" . . . loyal. He wants to go out with me. But my father . . . "

"He doesn't go for the relationship continuing."

"Right." Then she began to cry. "You understand. He saved my life. But my father is my father. What am I supposed to do?"

"What do you want to do, Alana?"

"I don't know. Ali wants to take me to The Fox."

"It's still your life."

Arrest scene: close-up of the red sneakers and two heavy pairs of black oxfords generally worn by policemen. A woman's house shoes attempting to get between the sneakers and the oxfords. One pair of oxfords heading off the house shoes, the other following the red sneakers out the door. Long shot from twenty-seventh floor: a black boy being flung into the back seat of a police car, a policeman slamming the door and getting into the passenger seat, his partner getting in the other side and driving away.

Unknown to Ali, the father blamed him for the incident rather then seeing him as the saviour of his daughter's life. He was less angered by the random crime itself than by the fact that his daughter had been out of the school building without permission. Because of my frequent visits to the hospital, Mr. Laing concluded that I could be trusted to keep a protective eye on Alana, in case, as he said, "interested parties try to take advantage of her condition." I suppose I should have said something to Mr. Laing on behalf of the interested party, but I didn't want the surveillance job handed over to someone else.

When Alana asked her father if she could go out with Ali, Mr. Laing decided upon direct action. He telephoned the young man. Ali came to see me on Monday, his mood alternating between anger and suicidal depression. Petulantly, he described their conversation.

" 'Nice young man,' he calls me. 'I appreciate what you did,' nice young man. 'But she's like a little girl in some ways now,' nice young man. I'm thinking to myself, 'You don't trust no black boy.' "

"You think he's a racist?"

"Sure, he's a fucking racist. 'Why would a sharp, sophisticated kid like you want to go out with her?' I will translate for you, Mr. Pender: 'It's not that I'm a racist.' Sure he's not."

"He probably wouldn't trust any boy with her now."

"Especially black boys. We're supposed to have uncontrollable sex drives, you know. So I told him: 'I see what you're getting at.' And he says, 'I thought you'd understand.' Except he's wrong, Mr. Pender. I love Alana."

"Did you tell him that?"

"Yes." His face expressed a sorrow I hope I never know. Then he returned to the petulant tone. " 'Love is all well and good,' nice young man, 'and so is loyalty, but it's time to give this relationship a rest.' Rest. He means rest in peace."

Alana knew nothing of this telephone call. Unfortunately, she remembered the date with Ali. Suddenly ignored by her boyfriend, she came to my room almost daily, leaving her increasingly frustrating schoolwork in her locker. Despite the grief she felt at losing Ali, she couldn't bring herself to blame him. "He must have felt he was too young," she tearfully concluded, "to consider spending his life with a handicapped person." While comforting her, I decided to interfere no further. I began to hope, like Mr. Laing, that time would heal her wound.

Spring came and finally the warm weather. Alana was desperate for release from her father's expectations and the drudgery of sitting with him over her homework until after midnight. She would come to school at the same time in the same old-fashioned outfits but would duck into the washroom and change into tight jeans. She began to walk around with one of those damned head-sets, and when I asked to listen, expecting maybe jazz or a Mozart sonata, I heard instead a shrill noise, like a construction site.

"You like it?" she asked with a dull smile. "It's Metallica." As she walked away, I wanted to cry, seeing she was now trying to turn herself into one of 'them.' Not until that moment had I fully realized what all of us had lost. Then I started thinking about a miracle, too.

Ali was in the seminar that afternoon. He often skipped class now and was usually morose when he did show up, occasionally lashing out at someone who gave a particularly stupid answer. I called him aside after the bell.

"Do you ever see Alana any more?" I asked.

"Around."

"You know what I mean."

"What's it to you?"

"I don't know. It's pretty quiet around here since the whole thing happened."

"Yeah."

I felt the waters and I knew the danger, but, still, I had to take the plunge. "She's heartbroken, you know. Why don't you just talk to her? She can still talk." Ali stared at me as if I had stuck a lemon into his mouth. He turned and began to walk away. Enraged, I said to his back, "That's right, just walk away. Pretend like nothing's happened. That behaviour seems to run in your family." You have to be very careful when you talk to a young person. I thought he might turn around like

Jason and try to slug me, but he just stopped momentarily and then continued out the door.

✧

The stories I heard about that fatal evening were fairly consistent. What I know first-hand is that Ali telephoned her and that Mr. Laing took the receiver and hung up on him. I know that later Ali came to their door, that Alana ran past her father into the street, and that the two of them ran off together. Mr. Laing called me, wanting to know where the kids hung out. I gave him a number of possibilities along with The Fox, hoping he would just stay home and wait it out. Fat chance.

He went directly to each place I gave him, finally arriving at The Fox, an old Toronto movie house with springs and stuffing coming out of the seats, sticky floors, and a pall of marijuana smoke. As usual, a horror film was on that night; the kids told me it was *Psycho*. I can see in my mind Mr. Laing entering this lurid place during the infamous shower scene. Alana, not knowing illusion from reality, is holding on to Ali for reassurance. She sees a familiar looking man in the aisle, walking backwards, staring into each row of teenagers, looking for something. As Janet Leigh's blood goes down the drain and the kids yell out "Awesome!," she feels Ali's lips on hers, their glasses clacking together. She can no longer see. Panic. She gasps and begins to struggle against her boyfriend.

"Don't!" he whispers in her ear. "It's your father!"

Understanding, she loses herself, allowing his supple tongue to slip between her lips, to explore the reaches of her mouth, her throat. Gratitude must have surged through her, gratitude that she was still alive and could feel such wonderful things.

"Alana!"

Her father called out her name in the theatre that night. And though many knew precisely where she sat, nobody said a word.

✧

The names Hazeltine and MacTavish, P.C. Hazeltine and Sergeant MacTavish, are now household words in Toronto. The two police officers were staking out an area along Brimley Road in order to nab a car thief. The area borders a fifty acre park with trees known as 'the woods.' A few years back, a developer proposed to use this land for yet another shopping mall. The residents of the area, among whom were hundreds of kids, came out to defeat the proposal. You might say the woods have paid the kids back, the evergreens and foliage providing them with both a love nest and a hiding place from the police. No one would go into the woods at night for any other reason.

Ali and Alana had passed by the woods together, thinking separate thoughts of the night it would be theirs. On the night in question, there were many lovers, but space was still available amongst the trees. I would like to think that Alana was no longer thinking of all the things she had failed to relearn, but of the joy of being young. Hell, she had a right to that much.

A rolling red light from a police car and the whoop of a siren brought everyone to his feet. The startled lovers straightened their clothes, threw away the drugs, and peered out from behind the trees.

Ali and Alana, who were near the border of the woods, saw the two policemen with flashlights intently chasing a small dark figure. At first, the fleeing youth darted between the trees with the sureness of a bat. But the rolling light disoriented him; he tripped over a root and struck his head on the base of a tree.

Constable Hazeltine roughly turned the boy over and shone the flashlight in his face. He pulled him to his feet and, keeping the light on him, revealed to Sergeant MacTavish and to all the kids behind the trees the face of Jason Carr.

"Resisting arrest, huh? Bloody little thief. This time you won't be getting off so easy."

The constable switched off the light and, in the next moment, the boy shrieked. Although no one could see, everyone heard the dull thud of the nightstick. Without hesitation, Ali stepped forward.

"Sir, don't hurt him."

The other flashlight shone on Ali's face.

"Who in hell are you?"

Alana then emerged from hiding. The light caught her as she stepped forward to stand beside Ali.

The police partners must have had a moment of *deja vu*, the three faces seeming so familiar. Then they remembered, having been on duty the day the brick fell.

The Sergeant asked, "You want to protect this lad, do you?" He shifted the flashlight on to Jason, now a sullen prisoner in red sneakers.

"Please don't hurt him, sir. That's all."

"Have you ever seen one of them with manners like this?" he asked his partner.

"Can't say that I have. Let's charge him with obstruction."

Ali must have felt the rage growing inside him, rising from his throat. He may not have seen the light on Alana's face nor heard the Sergeant ask, "You're Alana Laing, aren't you? There's a bulletin out on you. 'Missing female. May be disoriented.' "

"Two birds with one stone," quipped Constable Hazeltine.

"You!" the Sergeant snapped at Ali, once again shining the light on Jason and holding him by the collar. "You know who this is?" Then, as if reciting 'The House That Jack Built,' he continued. "This is the boy that threw the brick that crushed her head that fucked her life . . . ."

The Constable laughed at his partner's wit. The Sergeant then disregarded Jason and spoke to Ali. "We don't need any advice from the likes of you. In fact, we'd all be a helluva lot better off around here without the likes of you." And then he spoke beyond Ali and Alana directly to the woods. "Is there anyone back there who cares to disagree?"

No one has been able to tell me if Ali waited for an answer.

Climactic scene: A scream from Ali's mouth and then slo-mo of Ali's fist shattering the Sergeant's face and the Sergeant reeling backward, his hand groping for his gun holster. Ali coming toward him menacingly and a bullet from Constable Hazeltine's gun entering the young man's skull behind his ear. Ali falling forward, already dead.

Time to roll the credits on this nightmare, empty out the theatre, and clean up the mess. Trouble is I have to face that goddamned classroom every day without the two people I cared about the most.

After the funeral, I saw Ali's parents speaking to the Principal. The Principal pointed in my direction, so I assumed that I was the subject of their conversation. Sure enough, his parents walked over to me. Mr.

Rose removed his hat and his wife stood slightly behind him with that look of hard-won dignity on her face that Ali had described. The father said to me, "Mr. Pender, sir, I just wanted you to know how highly my son thought of you. He said you were more than a teacher to him, that you made him feel like a human being." I thanked him, shook his hand, expressed some meaningless condolence to them both, and walked off to sob in the privacy of my car.

Used to be that teaching was a more predictable sort of job, a group of students speaking the same language, sharing the same set of values, writing papers and exams, hello sir, goodbye sir, see you next year. Now they babble to each other in Chinese. Or they come in clanking chains, dressed for a gang war. Or they sit and stare at you as if you were a bathroom mirror. Christ, they even do their makeup! No opinions, no interest. Give them a grade, process them. Well, I'm no machine. I'm no entertainer, either, like some of these clowns, playing education for laughs or lecturing other teachers on the plastic chicken circuit. And you can count me out of the staff room football pools. Thanks but no thanks. I care about history and the state of this world and the way people treat each other. That's why I plan to retire early and do something that really matters.

REUNION

Songs to aging children come
Aging children, I am one
—*Joni Mitchell*

IT IS AUTUMN, A CLEAR, OVERLY warm November day in St. Louis, Missouri, and I, a rapidly greying man, early forties, am standing beside my older brother on a cinder running track facing a football field. It is homecoming weekend at my nephew's school. The young man, despite his heavy equipment and the heat of the day, canters by and waves to us proudly. Without warning, the band—no more than ten pieces—begins to play the alma mater slowly and slightly out of tune. Suddenly, I am crying, sobbing shamefully, squeezing shut my eyes and placing my nose into prayerfully clasped hands, though I am no alumnus of this school.

I have heard alma maters before, but never until this moment understood how they are written for the aging. The raggedy band continues on its dirgelike pace as I try to regain my composure. I am a Canadian now, with a university trained intellect. Is it body, soul, or both which have launched this in-house rebellion? Stop this foolish crying, turn back to the stands, and take your seat.

✧

My mother is seated in the shade of the balcony of her apartment in San Diego, the sun relentless in this desert-become-a-city. She stares into that cloudless blue sky. Cancer has begun its final assault upon her body. Were it I on that balcony with that diagnosis, I would be

125

contemplating my impending death. Or running around town looking for miracle cures.

My mother, beautiful as ever, hair dyed a silvery blonde, skin white and still smooth, sits entirely self-possessed. She is a woman who does not express doubt or seek advice. Since the day she left her family, she has been able to live by those beliefs most natural to her—foremost amongst them: dress well and always look your best. Her second husband, a humourless man whose perfectly aligned suede slippers wait patiently for him outside the door of the bathroom, is the opposite of her first husband. He is constantly showing my mother in so many little annoying ways how much he loves her.

I have spent almost thirty years waiting to ask her questions about her leaving home, letting one visit after another go by in craven silence. Even after surgery, she seemed so strong I was able to assure myself I had ample time. There are questions you do not ask from a sense of delicacy, others from a lack of courage. Poised now to join her on the balcony, I am impelled only by the urgency and finality of the moment.

❖

On a Friday morning, back when her hair was a volatile red, my mother served breakfast in her old housecoat—blue flowers on a white background. It always reminded me of a birthday cake. My father, placing the commuter's kiss on her cheek, left to catch the Long Island Railroad to Penn Station. On this day, she served something sweet—pancakes or French toast. I finished my milk. I brushed my teeth. My kiss was as unthinking as my father's had been. Out on the front porch I heard a scream. I rushed back inside and found my mother on the kitchen floor, propped on an elbow, weeping. I helped her to her feet. She kissed me, said she was all right, said I should go to school. It was just a slip on the floor.

That night, my father told me she had gone to Chicago for the weekend to see an old friend. I nodded, pretending to hear, though my mind was on a football game I was to play the next day, a Saturday game with cheerleaders and marching bands. At some point during that game, the field, the sky, the players, the referees all turned green.

From behind that sea of green, I could not tell the doctor the score of the game or what teams were playing.

I spent three days under observation. When my father picked me up at the hospital, she wasn't with him. Nor was she at home. I sat at my desk in my bedroom. My father was across the hall, lying on his bed reading the *New York Times*. It was October 1961. I was fifteen. I waited for my father to tell me what had happened.

Concussions are said to produce temporary states; yet now my entire life seemed to have changed.

✧

Tonight is a night for which I have trained intensively for three months, daily workouts amongst the old Jewish men at the health club in Toronto. My body has been punished into its best condition since high school. My skin is tanned, my clothes painstakingly selected. I get my hair styled the day I board the plane for New York. I imagine that everyone will be trying to look healthy, happy, and wealthy—everyone, that is, who will appear at my high school's twentieth reunion.

I have arranged to go to the affair with an old friend, Terry. Because our last names begin with the same letter, we shared every homeroom, many other classes, and countless experiences together outside of school. He picks me up at my father's house, forcing memories and associations to rocket out of control: the sad departure of the Giants and Dodgers which taught a whole generation that you can leave the people who love you; the birth of the Mets; my driver's license; Nathans; Jones Beach; the spice of freedom—wonderfully illusory and never again to be tasted.

The tape playing in the car turns back the clock for one sweet second. And then I remember how much I hate this town and most of the people who will be there tonight. I remember the cliques from which I was excluded and for whose full acceptance I would have cut my wrists.

✧

"Where's mother?"

He lowered *The Times* and stared over the top of his reading glasses. "I'll tell you the truth, Kenneth, I don't know."

"Didn't she go to Chicago?"

"No."

"So where is she, Dad?"

"Your mother's left me." That was it. Nothing more. No, he wasn't finished. "I've got a detective on it."

A detective? My father had hired a detective to trail my mother. My father would never again refer to her with any words other than "your mother."

Back in my room, crying, I remember how they'd battled through the years. From our beds, my brother and I would listen passively at first and then try to cover our ears, unlike my sister who often tried to get between them. The arguments would end with my mother threatening to leave. Then my father would bring two large suitcases up from the basement, as if to say, "Go ahead. See if I care." I would hear the suitcases clump down on the landing, I would hear my mother's tears. I saw now that my mother had simply chosen her own place and time.

My sister and brother were both away at college. Although we are close in age, we grew up as three only children. The foremost memory of my sister is her studying, straight-backed, a corona of lamplight around her black hair, building her house of bricks. In contrast, I always felt guilty at my own idleness. Fiercely intellectual, she learned that her best protection against fear and despair was ceaseless work. My brother took refuge in athletics, joining one violent sport after another to vent his anger and to avoid home. My escape was through fantasy, music, literature. My sister, my brother, and myself—a hard-working bank executive, an athletic coach, a writer. Three aging children, still wedded to the habits of childhood.

They called during the week but neither conversation shed any light on Mother's disappearance. Puzzlement and concern were in my siblings' voices, but we had never learned to talk to each other. Still, it was some comfort to know that they knew.

I returned to school. Somehow, I tried to lead a normal existence. Divorce was still illegal in New York; the worst marriages often stayed together. I boarded the school bus with great anxiety. No one appeared to know anything, not even my next-door neighbour who had boarded the bus with me. At school, everything seemed the same, better than the same. By Friday, people who never had much time for me were starting up conversations, and even some girls were paying attention.

The last year and a half at high school, while not the best of times, was better than the ostracism which I had previously endured. However, the fact that my more popular classmates merely talked to me was not enough. I never gained admittance to their inner circle. Despite the fact that my mother's absence from home freed me from the constant tension of bickering, I blamed her for having messed up my life, for everything that I should have been but wasn't.

✧

Three months after she left, I received a letter. My mother's handwriting was on the envelope. I was not resentful but thankful, so thankful.

> Dear Kenny,
> After many unpleasant years of life with your father, I met another man whom I have come to love very much and who loves me. I obtained a divorce in Mexico and have remarried. As you can see by the postmark, I now live in Houston. I know I have not been a real mother to you for some time, but I would like the opportunity to start again. Let us know if you would like to visit and we will be happy to make the necessary arrangements.
> Love,
> Mom

I moved quickly from thankfulness to outrage.

My sister was the first to visit. She assured me that Mother was very happy, but I took no comfort in her words. I felt an even greater distance than before from my sister, for whom these visits seemed significant. In my view, Mother had to pay for both her inconsiderateness and her misdeed. I arranged a brief visit but made it clear that she had lost her right to act as a mother, fitting retribution after all. Whatever need for a mother that drove my sister did not drive me.

✧

I go out on the porch. A wind has made the afternoon cooler and more comfortable.

"God, it's nice out here," I begin.

"I love it," she says. "I love life. I often think how healthy I am but for this illness. I've felt no pain and discomfort except for the operations and the treatments. Sometimes it's hard to believe I really have cancer."

"It must be hard." How feeble! Is that all I can say? "Mom, you mind if we talk? There's something I've been wanting to ask you for a long time."

"Yes? Why don't you sit down?"

Her strength of mind is simultaneously comforting and disconcerting. Where is the vulnerability one would expect in a dying person? I sit across from her, but she motions for me to move next to her. "When you left home—and really I wouldn't be surprised if you couldn't remember this; it was twenty-five years . . ."

"I remember. Of course I remember." She remembers everything, even the way I used to scratch my back on the door post.

"Why didn't you leave any of us a note? Why didn't you leave me a note?"

"Yes, I might have done that. It seems obvious now. But at the time, it didn't. I'd been trapped so long, I had to get away as quickly . . . as possible."

"Quickly and cleanly."

"All right, but I did wait until you kids were grown up." She puts a hand on my arm. "Why haven't you told me this before?"

"Here I was, fifteen years old, and one day my mother disappears."

"I'm sorry. If it does any good to say it, I'm sorry." And what else can she say to her aging child? That he might have enjoyed more of her lightness and grace and humour and strength if he'd allowed himself to be less angry and resentful?

✧

Why have I come to this reunion? Simply because something inside me needs all of them to know how successful I am. Every conversation is meant to dazzle, is twisted, turned, and falsified in order to reflect a bright light on the teller. It is an evening of double monologues in which one feels no joy, only a cruel glee in having left others behind. After a full two hours of boasting, I am sated. My mouth hurts. Finally, I grab some food from what's left of the buffet and sit with Terry.

"You certainly seem to be enjoying yourself tonight."

"I just wanted to show those people that I'm not as stupid as they thought I was."

Terry smiles, savouring the irony. "You wanted to show how much better you are than them."

"I did. I guess I never got over hating them because of the way they excluded me. It's hard to outgrow that kind of thing."

He nods. There is something in that statement which is true for him as well.

"You remember junior year?" I ask. "You have no idea what a time that was for me. I guess no one but you even knew that my mother had left home."

He smiles. "Do you really think for a minute that your neighbour was about to let such gossip escape him?"

It is a Swedish meatball that crash-lands along with my fork. The mild social flowering which occurred at the end of high school was something more than my resentful mind could understand. Knowing my pain, those I hated had treated me with more kindness than I deserved.

◆

As the alma mater draws to a close, I sneak a look at my brother. He is moved by something as well. Perhaps it is the pride he feels in his fine son. I take an enormous breath.

Mother, country, family, reunion, homecoming—all the trappings of sentiment. I know it is not proper to give in to such feelings, especially in our era. But what if, for a moment, standing in the city where the great rivers meet, I just let go and allow them to lead me back to that true self which has stood beside me, ignored for all these years? I would say, "I miss you. Home, family, friends, I miss you."

The major chords of the music, strong, deep, and sorrowful, sweep through me, singing of the people and the land that will never again be the same for me.

❖

Joining hands with my brother and sister over my mother's deathbed, I see her face, like her hair, silvery pale as the moon, as the winged-god Mercury or Lady Liberty herself. What *Who's Who* does she appear in? What was on the list of major accomplishments in her life? How had she tried to impress others, except as one who had the courage to live as she saw fit? If I had allowed myself to feel then as I do now, I would have said for her to hear, "Mother, I love you."

KEN KLONSKY is a behavioural resource teacher who has worked with adolescents in the Toronto area since 1982. His fiction has appeared in *This Magazine* and *Education Forum*. His play *Taking Steam*, co-written by Brian Shein, was published by Playwrights Canada. He moved to Vancouver in 1992.

NEW AND RECENT TITLES FROM
ARSENAL PULP PRESS

The Bride of Doctor Tin   *Fiction/Tom Walmsley*
A sequel to the groundbreaking 1979 novel *Doctor Tin*: an uncompromising and frenzied descent into a sensual world, in which nothing is barred but the rules. *ISBN 0-88978-254-7; $11.95*

Canada Remapped   *Non-Fiction/Scott Reid*
If Quebec separates, what then? An examination of the potentially explosive issue of the partition of a post-Confederation Quebec, and how the federal government is currently unprepared for such a scenario. *ISBN 0-88978-249-0; $14.95*

Higgledy Piggledy   *Fiction/Robin Skelton*
An entertaining collection of short stories dealing with the supernatural, informed by the razor-sharp wit of the author, Canada's most famous male witch. *ISBN 0-889798-247-4; $13.95*

The Imaginary Indian   *Non-Fiction/Daniel Francis*
A fascinating and revealing history of the "Indian" image mythologized by Canadian culture since 1850, propagating stereotypes of the "noble savage" that exist to this day. *ISBN 0-88978-251-2; $15.95*

The Production of the World   *Non-Fiction/Stephen Osborne*
A meditation on family and community, on the imperative of occupying a moral universe, on marginality and the sweetness of life. *ISBN 0-88978-259-8; $11.95*

Available at your favourite bookstore, or directly prepaid (add $1.00 per book for postage plus 7% GST in Canada) from:

         ARSENAL PULP PRESS
         100-1062 Homer Street
         Vancouver, BC V6B 2W9

Write for our free catalogue.